Sauce of Life

A Novel

Tan Kheng Yeang

Order this book online at **www.trafford.com**
or email orders@trafford.com

Most Trafford titles are also available at major online book retailers.

First published in Malaya, 1974
Copyright 1974 by Tan Kheng Yeang

Printed in the United States of America.

ISBN: 978-1-4269-7402-1 (sc)
ISBN: 978-1-4269-7403-8 (hc)
ISBN: 978-1-4269-7404-5 (e)

Library of Congress Control Number: 2011910913

Trafford rev. 04/02/2012

www.trafford.com

North America & International
toll-free: 1 888 232 4444 (USA & Canada)
phone: 250 383 6864 • fax: 812 355 4082

Other books by the same author

Fiction

Novels
Conflict in the Home
Struggle Toward Extinction
Motivating Forces

Poetry
Diverse Modes
Poems (Flowery Country/Sun and Rain/Grains of Sand)

Non-Fiction

Memoir
Dark Days

Philosophy
Intrinsic to Universe
The Material Structure

Sayings
Reduced Reflections

Linguistics
LUIF: A New Language
LUIF Dictionaries

To

Seang Lin and Seang Beng

The author wishes to thank Ms. Chao Wei Yang and Ms. Valerie Cameron for their invaluable assistance in preparing the manuscript of this book for publication.

Lai Pek is a self-made man and proud of it. He has reached middle age as a successful businessman and patriarch of a thriving family. His outlook on life is smug, self-satisfied, and complacent. However, no one goes through life unscathed, and, like a tiger silently creeping through the jungle, adversity stalks Lai Pek, striking swiftly.

Faced with a formidable business rival, a horrifying tragedy at his rubber plantation, and a shocking crime that threatens the lives of those dear to him, Lai Pek must reassess his values and draw on an inner strength that he may not possess if he is to survive the crises that life has thrown at him.

Set in a small town in peninsular Malaya in the 1930's, the story takes place against the colourful backdrop of the lives and customs of the Chinese denizens and the inexorable encroachment of modern ideas and influences on their long-held values and ways of life.

Contents

Chapter 1

The Shop

"These shoes," said the customer, sitting on a chair and endeavouring to insert his right foot into one of a pair of black shoes, "do not fit at all. Haven't you got another size?"

"Certainly we have," replied Lai Pek, and he ordered his assistant to take down from the top of a lofty case a particular pair of leather shoes, which he indicated with his finger. The counter was strewn with a motley array of footwear, for the customer was very critical in his choice—extremely trying, in fact, but Lai Pek remained as urbane and smiling as ever.

"This pair is about right," the customer graciously commented, after trying on first the right shoe and then the left for five minutes. "How much?"

"Only twelve dollars and fifty cents," was the answer.

"Ridiculous! Eight dollars would be the correct price."

"Ai-ya!" exclaimed Lai Pek. "If I do trade on such terms, it won't be long before I have to close up shop."

"Well, then, state the exact amount you want."

"What I have just quoted is the usual price. But in consideration of the fact that you have been here twice or thrice before, I will give them to you for eleven dollars. Not a cent less," he said, a decisive inflection in his voice.

"Come," said the customer, "nine dollars and a half."

"I am afraid that I cannot oblige you." He was prepared to give them for ten dollars, but there was no reason, he thought, why he should not angle for more. He could easily discern that the man was loath to part with the shoes. "The price I ask is fair."

The customer assumed a stout resolve he did not feel and slowly walked out the door. Lai Pek watched him depart with an equal exhibition of firmness but with an eye on his movements, ready to call the customer back before he reached the pillar at the side of the house and vanished from sight. This was not fated to happen, however, for the customer turned back and reluctantly counted out the sum required.

Bustling about, wearing an amiable expression upon his vigilant countenance, Lee Lai Pek was the very embodiment of prosperous fussiness. His heart sang, because business was good and the day had been exceptionally lucky. He smiled as he pondered over the morning's profits and beamed a more joyous smile as he remembered the stranger who had entered his shop just before noon. Daydreaming does not yield a good cash return, and he seldom indulged in this luxury, but a look of contemplation stole into his eyes as he speculated on the stranger's position—apparently a wealthy man, judging from his spontaneous order for a considerable stock of goods, without the customary amount of bargaining.

Lai Pek was plainly apparelled (he was by no means particular with regard to dress and personal appearance in general) in a long-sleeved shirt with brown and greenish stripes, closely buttoned at the neck and wrists, that hung over his loose gray trousers, which were not adorned with any pockets at all.

His feet were encased in a pair of slippers that had seen long service but had not quite reached the end of their usefulness.

He was a man who had attained that period of life that is usually associated with the meridian of success, especially in commerce—to be more specific, he had reached the age of forty-five. He did not exceed ordinary stature or ordinary weight; this latter point was somewhat remarkable, as experience usually demonstrates that an increasing prosperity also begets an increasing abdomen. Lai Pek seemed to be surrounded by a soothing aura of indestructible prosperity, and his appearance was stamped with an indelible impression of a strenuous purpose successfully fulfilled. He did not assume any particular airs, but one could form that impression, especially by looking at his smiling countenance.

His eyes were the shrewdest imaginable, and he possessed a peculiar habit. When he spoke, he directed his gaze not straight at a person's face but towards his chest, as if he were lost in a profound study of the pattern and fabric of his coat. Although he did not look steadily at a person's face, nevertheless Lai Pek contrived to notice every expression on it. His politeness was of remarkable magnitude, and this was indicated by the bland smile he usually wore.

As he sat perched behind his counter that sultry afternoon, during a lull in the business, an individual entered.

"Greetings, Lai Pek," said the man in an appropriate tone, bowing pleasantly.

"Welcome, Hwey Pin," returned Lai Pek in a pleasingly cordial voice, at the same time rising up and bending his body just as elegantly. "How are you?"

"Very well."

"Please sit down. Have a cup of tea?"

"A thousand thanks. Don't inconvenience yourself."

Soh Hwey Pin seated himself and grasped the proffered cup with both hands. He was a short, heavy man of about Lai Pek's age, and he wore a dark suit. The coat, not too noteworthy for cleanliness, was totally unbuttoned, partly on account of the heat and partly because it was inconveniently tight, but no vestige of a shirt could be seen under it. His head was crowned with a quantity of tousled, dry hair, and his forehead bulged prominently. His unpleasing countenance suggested an unscrupulous disposition. As he mopped his cheeks with a handkerchief, he remarked, "Old Loh Hwai had another big loss today. He has failed so systematically for so long now that he is absolutely ruined."

"Poor fellow!" said Lai Pek sympathetically. "But the trouble with him is he has no sound practical sense." He added, in a tone implying a consciousness of his own superiority in that regard, "As it is aptly said, 'if you plant gourds, you obtain gourds; beans, you obtain beans.' He is not careful in what he does."

"Quite right," stated Hwey Pin.

"How has this new disaster come upon him?"

"He has been giving a great deal of credit indiscriminately. One of his debtors, Pa See, has secretly sold his shop and absconded this morning—where? Only Heaven knows."

"I remember the person, although I haven't had any business dealings with him. A great rogue he is—so he has gone off? I am not surprised. I was sure when I first met him some years ago—he approached me on some matter I have forgotten now—that he would be up to mischief one of these days," observed Lai Pek, with the air of a soothsayer whose predictions have duly come to pass.

"Yes, he is a bad man. It is strange how Loh Hwai could trust him—quite surprising."

"As for me," smiled Lai Pek, "I judge whether a person is trustworthy first, before I allow him to owe anything. Besides, debts must be kept within reasonable bounds." He paused for some time to look at a stranger who had entered the shop and then immediately went out again to inspect the ditch. "I am curious to know how Loh Hwai contrived to earn his money. I should have thought he was quite incapable of it."

"Well, money is not necessarily obtained only by brains. Chance can do the trick just as well. When he first came to Lanta some fifteen years ago, business happened to be very brisk, and due to undeserved fortune, he managed to be prosperous. It was a miracle that he was not plunged into ruin long ago, but luck is luck," concluded Hwey Pin sagely.

He rose and poured out another cup of tawny tea; after imbibing the soothing beverage in measured gulps, he again sat and said, "By the way, Lai Pek, I have called to settle your account for last month."

"Yes; what is the amount?" He was extremely averse to giving away money for any reason.

Receiving the reply, Lai Pek unwillingly approached the safe and took out the necessary sum to pay Hwey Pin, who kept a grocery from which Lai Pek's household was daily supplied with provisions. Hwey Pin was also a sort of broker, acting as intermediary between two persons, usually strangers, who desired to purchase or sell a rubber estate or house. Whenever a transaction was fortunate enough to reach a successful conclusion, he obtained an estimable commission for his services, thereby substantially aiding both his bank account and his satisfaction.

After inserting the money in a large brown purse, which was then deposited in his coat pocket, Hwey Pin casually observed, "I remember, Lai Pek, you told me last month that you had some spare money and would like to buy a rubber estate."

"True. I see no way of employing it in my business, and as rubber, I understand, is yielding such a handsome profit, I am thinking of making a venture into it." A keen and bold look crept into his eyes, the look of speculation, and he basked in the luxurious feelings of a traveller about to behold the wonders of a strange country. "Have you come across a good estate lately?"

"Yes, I have found just the thing for you. It is a very excellent one, about thirty acres."

"Where is it situated?"

"At Chola, hardly twenty-five miles from here."

"What is the price?"

"Just six hundred dollars per acre."

"That is rather high."

"Not at all, considering the fine income obtainable at present. As a matter of fact, it is quite cheap. It is a very, very good estate indeed. The owner is forced to sell it because of money troubles. Most persons would try to retain it," said Hwey Pin, with a tongue profusely lubricated with oil.

"Who is the owner?" inquired Lai Pek with deep interest.

"I don't think you know him. His name is Pang Tit, and he lives in Lomai. He used to be prosperous, but he was so extravagant that he is now involved in a financial maze. He recently told a friend of mine that he wished to sell the piece of land, if he could obtain a reasonable price. That's how I came to hear of it. I have since seen him, and I can say he will not prove hard to deal with," replied Hwey Pin with a benevolent expression.

Lai Pek was very much gratified to learn that the proprietor was a soft person in trouble, for he scented a good bargain.

"I think," he said after a pause, "that we had better go and examine it first. If it is to my liking, then we can proceed to discuss terms with him."

"Quite right. We must fix a day when we are both free. What day will be convenient for you?"

"Let me see. Today is Tuesday—we'll go on Friday, if it suits you."

"Very good. Shall I call for you at nine o'clock in the morning? It is better not to go too late, or it will be unpleasantly hot."

"I agree."

"I must go now. Don't escort me."

"When you have leisure, come and have another chat."

After they had executed a ceremonious bow and expressed the hope of seeing each other again, Hwey Pin departed in the best of spirits.

Comfortably installed behind the counter, Lai Pek cast long, appraising stares at the commodities, assessing those that needed replenishing. The offerings were of various sorts and were arrayed with exemplary care in glass cases. Luxuriant assortments of magnificent silk and cotton cloth, small cardboard boxes of buttons and ribbons, books and writing materials, crockery, culinary utensils, and a generous collection of tins of diverse shapes and sizes, exhibiting on their labels such tempting items as biscuits, lichees, and sardines, formed the stock.

The principal furnishings of the spacious store included the counter; a round table on which conveniently reposed the inevitable pot of tea (most invaluable of beverages!) and a tray with some cups; half a dozen cane chairs; a desk appropriated to the clerk's use and littered with ledgers and papers, to say nothing of a slab with a stick of ink, an abacus and some brushes; a formidable iron safe; an eight-day clock with a circular dial disproportionate in size to the rest of its structure; and some ornamental prints on the walls.

After the final rush in the evening, business became slacker, and only a few stragglers crossed the threshold now and then. The shop would close at eight, but for the last three or four hours it did not necessarily require Lai Pek's personal attention, so he usually retired and returned only at closing time for a few minutes to see that everything was properly settled for the night. During this interval, his employees were left to work by themselves; they totalled eight, including a clerk, six salesmen, and a boy who officiated in the capacity of general servant. As he was now hungry after his restless exertions, he withdrew behind the partition separating the shop from the rest of the house and entered the parlour.

Chapter 2

The Problem of Marriage

The large oblong chamber presented to his view a scene of merriment and confusion, for the family was gathered there to await the evening meal. His wife was holding an uproarious conversation with a friend, who then rose and took her departure by the back door. Mrs. Lee accompanied her to the doorstep, where they talked for another five enjoyable minutes. She was about four years younger than her husband and had been married to him when not quite seventeen. Since then she had borne him five children, although the couple wished that they had more—fertility and offspring increased a person's respectability and was an incontestable omen of Heaven's protection. They had, on the whole, lived a happy and comfortable life together, though their double career was chequered with some slight matrimonial squabbles, which happened long before the commencement of this story and need not be chronicled. She had been on a round of visits and had returned only about an hour ago.

Their eldest son, Sum Goh, a young man of some twenty-two years, a teacher in a school, had also just come back from performing some additional work outside the usual school hours. He was lying in a long chair near a window to recuperate his energies, which had been profusely expended. He was an ordinary youth, of ordinary tastes and ordinary thoughts—he would not deviate from his conventional way of life for any consideration in the world. He read comic papers and the local newspaper at his club, to which he directed his steps, or rather his bicycle, every night. He heartily enjoyed the cinema, was a frequenter of fields dedicated to sport, did his work well, and was absolutely contented with his lot in life. He was not yet married, as he was in no hurry to do so and had given little thought to it. Furthermore, his parents were hypercritical in their tastes and had been on the lookout for a suitable bride for him since he was eighteen; though matchmakers had presented themselves by the dozen to enthusiastically recommend the marriageable girls within their acquaintance, they were forced to retire, discouraged and chagrined.

Their second child was a girl of seventeen who had left school scarcely a year ago and who was naturally grave and unsophisticated, although not averse to gaiety at home. The other three children, who were shouting joyously in play, were aged respectively eleven, seven, and five. The youngest was a girl and the two others boys.

Dinner was piled on the table, and it steamed deliciously. Lai Pek and his eldest son sat down and were soon ardently exercising their powers of mastication. While the former was helping himself to a piece of fried fish, holding it on the end of his chopsticks and preparing to chew with it a mouthful of rice, his wife remarked, "During the course of the afternoon, I thought I would like to pay a visit to Mrs. Loh Hwai, whom I have not seen for some considerable time. I went and found her alone and—what do you think?—she had, shortly before my arrival, been having a bitter quarrel with her husband. I never heard that they had ever been on anything but the best of terms before. But among her many just causes for complaint, she informed me with anger that her husband was useless in trade and that he had permitted himself to be cheated of ..."

"Oh, yes," interrupted Lai Pek, "I heard the story from Hwey Pin just a short while ago. But what can you do?" he continued, waving his left hand as if to clinch the irrefutable argument. “Some men must be foolish and some must be wise, if trade is to be carried on.” He directed his gaze to a bowl of pork soup, laid down his chopsticks, and drank three copious spoonfuls in rapid succession.

“I am sure,” chimed in Sum Goh, “that I do not think the worse of him for it. He must be of a kindly, trustful disposition.”

“What are you talking about?” retorted his father, with a look of disdain for his son’s fantastic ignorance. “He possesses a trustful disposition? I should think he does! But there is nothing praiseworthy I know of in that.” He coughed, as he was nearly choked by the ridiculous suggestion. “In trade, if success is to be more than a dream, the wisest maxim to put into practise is to be suspicious of everyone and trust a person only when the reasons are very good.” He looked around to impress this profound philosophy on his unenlightened family.

“I am afraid that I can’t believe that suspicion is a necessity. Why should it exist? Can there be no business without it?” persisted the obstinate Sum Goh.

“Of course not!” exclaimed Lai Pek quickly, as if someone were attacking his dearest treasure. “What is the supreme end and aim of life? Happiness! And how can you obtain any happiness at all if you have no money? And the best means of making money is trade, as everybody knows. Now, what is trade? It is the exchanging of money and goods; the more money you can get out of others, the better. What man can be such a fool, therefore, as not to take any money he can get out of you? And what does he care whether you can trust him or not, as long as he obtains the most important thing!” Here he bestowed a look of sublime wisdom on his sadly benighted son; then he slowly turned his attention to a plate of preserved cucumber, of which he took a mouthful, smacking his lips with satisfaction.

The youngest boy, Sum Liu, cried out loudly because his brother, Sum Chee, had inflicted a disagreeable box on his ear. The elders turned round, and Mrs. Lee exclaimed, "What are you crying about, Sum Liu?"

"Second brother has hit me," blubbered the boy.

"What did you hit him for, Sum Chee?" continued the mother.

"Why did he keep on pinching me? I don't like this," replied the one addressed, with a sullen look on his face.

"Silence! You wicked boy!" shouted Lai Pek. "You are always a liar. You like the touch of a bamboo stick. If you don't take care, you'll soon get what you want."

Sum Liu ceased crying, and harmony again prevailed.

"As for Mrs. Loh Hwai," began Mrs. Lee anew, "I sincerely pity her. She is so good and gentle a person that no trouble should ever alight on her."

"Trouble, like so many other products of Destiny, does not distinguish between good and bad persons," observed Sum Goh, philosopher *pro tem*, sententiously. After this exalted reflection, he applied himself to his plate once more.

"The fact that trouble has always existed, and will always exist, in this world," stated Lai Pek, "is as natural and right as sunshine. If there were no trouble at all, we would lose half our satisfaction in our good fortune. If everybody were happy and successful, there would be no particular cleverness in keeping trouble at a safe distance." This dictum was so impressive that neither Mrs. Lee nor Sum Goh had a word to offer in reply.

"After I left Mrs. Loh Hwai's," said Mrs. Lee, resuming her remarks, "I proceeded to Mrs. Boh Siu's, where I found a great number of people gathered to congratulate her on her sixtieth birthday. Many of her relatives were present, who had come from other places. I noticed particularly a certain Mrs. Sin Beng Hu, a young and charming person. Her husband is wealthy, and it seems that they have just come to stay in Lanta."

"What sort of a person is he?" inquired Lai Pek.

"I did not make a special study of his appearance," was the reply, "but he could not be much more than thirty years old. He was serious in appearance, had a square face, and was scrupulously dressed."

"Perhaps he is the person who came and bought some things at our shop this morning," exclaimed Lai Pek. "I hope he will become a regular customer of ours. He will bring us a great deal of profit," he concluded, with a note of undisguised satisfaction in his voice.

By that time he had finished his copious meal, winding it up with half a bowl of tea, which he drained at one gulp. Then he slowly rose and proceeded towards the kitchen to wash his mouth; returning, he settled himself in a cane chair, and, holding a long pipe in his hand, he enjoyed to repletion the pleasures of tobacco, contentedly puffing out thick clouds of smoke, which curled delightfully about his complacent countenance.

A short while afterwards, the other members of the family sat down to dinner, for the rule prevailed that they should not all eat at the same time; instead, they did so in successive batches. The table was cleared, and fresh dishes were served—a process which consumed some time—before the next group commenced their repast. Sum Goh had dispatched his victuals considerably earlier than his venerable parent. He habitually ate with respectable speed and rarely filled himself excessively, because he possessed a taste for swallowing various odds and ends at intervals during the course of the day, with the consequence that his appetite was greatly diminished at the regular meals. He was now installed in a cosy armchair, with one leg comfortably crossed over the other in a graceful attitude; he unfolded an illustrated sports weekly, which, judging from his animated face, he read with immense appreciation.

For a considerable period of time silence prevailed in the room, and all seemed to have found something to engage their attention. Lai Pek was apparently steeped in profound meditation, of a character impenetrable to an observer. Then Mrs. Lee, endowed with a constitutional intolerance for lack of discourse for any measurable interval, suddenly remarked, "I think it is time Sum Goh is married. I have a suitable girl in mind, just the right person—nothing to beat her."

She paused for an instant to take a pinch of sambal to mix with her food before continuing. Her words were electric—they immediately roused Lai Pek from reverie and Sum Goh from his reading.

"Yes! She is very charming indeed!" reiterated Mrs. Lee leisurely.

"Who is she?" inquired Lai Pek, an anxious expression on his face. "I hope she is of a good family."

"She certainly is," replied his genial spouse. "You are not going to insult me by supposing I don't possess the intelligence to distinguish between desirable and undesirable people?"

"Well, then, who have you in mind? You are very slow in imparting that valuable piece of information," said the exasperated Lai Pek sarcastically. "Promptitude in speech is a most precious asset, I should think," he added with ponderous emphasis.

"She is the youngest daughter of Ooi Soo Giat," responded Mrs. Lee calmly, without any further delay, not desiring to contradict her husband's advice. "She is just eighteen years old, pretty, and blessed with all the amiable characteristics."

"I am not personally acquainted with Ooi Soo Giat and we have not had any business interaction whatsoever, as the line he deals in is not mine," remarked Lai Pek, giving more of his attention to the problem of the father than the daughter. "But from reputation, he is a respectable man of good standing. He is said to possess quite a fair amount of wealth, and I have no objection to a family alliance with him."

"We must get hold of Mrs. Ka Soh to approach him about the affair. She could arrange the match satisfactorily. I think Ooi Soo Giat would not object to the marriage between his daughter and our son. The best time for the marriage to take place, if everything turns out all right, would be somewhere at the beginning of next year," said Mrs. Lee.

While this interesting conversation passed between his venerable parents, Sum Goh was perfectly silent. He listened with respectful attention but interjected no word of his own. His countenance bore a faint smile, tinged with some uneasiness, as the discussion progressed. His mother turned to him and said, "We have now found an excellent bride for you, Sum Goh. I am sure you will be very glad."

"I don't think I would like to marry at present," replied Sum Goh. "I wish you would drop this proposal. There is still time enough to talk about marriage later on."

Both his parents' faces registered immense surprise.

"What are you talking about!" exclaimed Lai Pek angrily. "How old do you think you want to be before you get married? Most men are married before your age, if their parents can afford it. You know you are the eldest son, and it's your duty to continue your honourable line without further delay."

"Remember, my son," chimed in Mrs. Lee sweetly, "you must seize the first opportunity you can. Good girls are not to be had at every street corner, you know; if you don't marry this time, you may never be able to get hold of another at all."

"The fact is," replied Sum Goh uneasily, "I don't mind marrying, but I have never seen this girl. I don't know whether I love her or not. I want to marry only the girl I choose."

His parents looked at each other for a speechless moment, as they had never heard their son give vent to such sentiments before.

For some time they were too paralyzed to speak. Lai Pek slowly recollected his faculties and stated, "So that's the reason you don't want to marry at present. You want to choose your own bride. You think that I and your mother are two old fools who don't know what's good for their son. You think we are trying to tyrannize you, I suppose?"

"I don't think anything of the sort," responded Sum Goh, more uneasy than before. He pretended to cast a glance at his paper.

"What has come over you I can't, for the life of me, think," declared Lai Pek peevishly. "Here we are, going to all sorts of trouble to find a bride for you, and you, instead of being glad, resent what you think of as our interference. Let me tell you—in my time, a young man would have been immensely glad if his parents had chosen a wife for him as soon as possible."

"Well, Sum Goh," chimed in Mrs. Lee, "of course, we have nothing but your welfare at heart. Wouldn't it have been ridiculous if, after having borne and bred you with tenderness and care through so many years, we should ultimately try to do something contrary to your best interests? It is only because you are our dear son that we have taken all this trouble about your marriage. If you were not, what would we care whom you marry?"

"I know all this very well," said Sum Goh, "and I do not like going against your wishes. But what you think suitable need not necessarily fit in with my choice. Every man has his own mind, his own judgment."

"There is only one good and one bad," retorted Lai Pek majestically. "When a person is good, he is good, no matter if a thousand persons may think to the contrary. And when a person is bad, he is bad, in spite of all that those who are partial to him can say. Take this girl we are discussing—either she is good and desirable or bad and undesirable. If you and your parents think differently, either you or we are wrong. The question comes down to this: is it more probable that you are right or we are right—you, who are barely emerged from life and know nothing whatever about the world, or we, who are old and experienced and possess more mature judgment?"

"But this question about the worth of the girl has nothing to do with the matter," said Sum Goh. "It does not follow that because a girl is possessed of all sorts of virtues and graces, a man must love her. A man can only love a girl according to his fancy."

"I think you must have been seeing the cinema too often," retorted Lai Pek.

Sum Goh looked at his venerable parent for a brief second with something like anger on his face then he blushed and looked down at his paper once more.

"I now know the reason for your unfilial opposition," continued Lai Pek. "You want to be modern and fashionable, and what you call love seems to be the most popular fashion at present prevailing. I am not ignorant of the fact that many young men think as you do, but I thought that a son of mine would have greater common sense than to follow the crowd. Listen to a word of advice before you rush headlong into ruin: what you think is modern may be modern to the Chinese, but it is not modern in the world. What has prevailed in the West for centuries cannot be called modern. The trouble with so many of us is that we imagine that everything imported from the West is new. If the Westerners were to adopt Chinese civilization, it would be just as modern to them. Because of our craze for modernism, we embrace everything, irrespective of whether it is good or bad. A thing is not going to be good just because it is modern. Just as I told you before, a thing is either good or bad. It can't change its value according to time, so long as it does not change its nature. A thing that is old now was new once; that which is new now will become old some day. If it is to be considered good when it's new and bad when it's old, this means that it has no real worth in itself. Time does not change gold into iron," he concluded pithily.

Mrs. Lee smiled approvingly at her husband's impressive discourse and cast apprehensive glances at her son to see if it had any effect on him but, though he looked uncomfortable, he did not seem to be abandoning his views; he did not change his recalcitrant attitude.

After an imperceptible pause Lai Pek resumed. "As for your saying that one can only love a girl according to one's fancy, this is all nonsense. To say that there is something inborn, something special, in a girl that draws you irresistibly to her is absurd. The thing for which you love her must be some quality in her that appeals to you; and there is no quality that exists in only one person. It may be rare, but it is common to a certain number of persons, if only you observe carefully. And let me tell you, you are committing a supreme folly if you love a girl blindly; you must marry her only for certain definite, admirable qualities in her. She must be chosen with great care."

"That is exactly what we have done!" exclaimed Mrs. Lee with evident triumph in her voice.

"We have selected an excellent girl for you; you will conceive a great affection for her after you are married. You are certain to, for any sensible man is sure to love excellence. You will live a happy life. I am convinced that our ancestors lived a much happier married life than the modern people who marry for love. They never had so many unfortunate divorces, like today. They never had such undesirable tragedies as those that are indispensably connected with love. Marriage is one of the many activities of life; there are other things to consider, and a man would be a fool to ruin himself for that alone."

"That is quite right," chimed in Mrs. Lee. "You remember the case of Ooi Kaw. He eloped with a girl last year because his parents wanted him to marry another girl. They were very angry and disowned him. The marriage did not prove a success; for, after living in dire poverty for a few months, they quarrelled and separated. Because he opposed his parents' choice and preferred to rely on his own judgment, his marriage turned out a failure, and he had to eat the bitter. The reason is he did not know how to select his wife properly but married her because he thought her fascinating."

Sum Goh listened to the parental exhortations in respectful silence, and finally he said, "You may or may not be right, but I am not interested in marriage at present. I wish you would drop the subject. There is still plenty of time for me to consider the problem."

His father heaved a sigh.

"It's useless arguing with you," he stated. "One might as well attempt to convince a stone about anything. All right. I am not attempting to force my will upon you, and I don't want you to feel that you are suffering horrible injury at my hands."

"It's a pity," sighed Mrs. Lee, loath to give up her idea. "Such a nice girl. What about our striking up an acquaintance with Ooi Soo Giat and his family? Our families will visit one another as much as possible. You can then decide, Sum Goh."

"And I suppose that Ooi Soo Giat's daughter is not one of those modern girls who want to choose their own husbands. She may not love him," said Lai Pek, in not the pleasantest of tones.

"I am sure they will love each other," responded Mrs. Lee fatuously.

Sum Goh did not utter a word, but his demeanour plainly indicated that he was averse to the suggestion.

Mrs. Lee found it futile to pursue the subject further; she muttered something audible only to herself and relapsed into silence. Lai Pek dismissed the matter from his mind and became absorbed in his thoughts once more. Sum Goh rose and left the room.

Chapter 3

The Theatre

That night Lai Pek thought about the theatre. He was not a devotee of the stage, regarding its frivolities with contempt and its incorrigible addicts as profligates of a ludicrous disposition, absolutely devoid of any sterling business sense. But occasionally he loved to see a play of the traditional type, depicting some glamorous incident from history.

He had a passionate fondness for the Chinese historical romances, in which he implicitly believed. He never stopped to question whether certain events could have happened; the more wonderful they were, the more interesting they became. Providing entertainment, these novels were a tremendous boon to the people. They never got weary of listening to the same marvellous tales told innumerable times and would gather in crowds around professional storytellers, who would retell episodes for a small charge. Immediately after dusk arrived, and as soon as their evening rice was consumed, devotees would hurry to the usual meeting places, which might occupy an empty space by the side of the road, the five-foot way, or some corner of a field, where they sat on benches around a small wooden table. The storyteller, with a pot of tea at hand to stimulate his voice and a well-thumbed volume spread out before him, read and explained the contents by the feeble light of a kerosene lamp; occasionally embellishing the recorded narrative from his own imagination, he spoke in a sonorous, eloquent voice, aided by suitable gestures. How absorbed the listeners were! The stories served a commendable purpose; the people acquired knowledge of history, although it might not be conspicuous for accuracy. The listeners automatically imbibed a portion of the spirit that pervaded the novels—the spirit of endurance in adversity—for they were on the side of the right. Enraptured, listeners immersed themselves in magnificent accounts of the multifarious trials and afflictions of virtuous heroes, who later emerged in exhilarating triumph, to the vast consternation of their foes, the villains.

Lai Pek hailed the nearest rickshaw.

"How much to the Teong Hua Theatre?" he demanded in a pompous voice.

"Forty cents," replied the puller.

Now, rickshaw-pullers were endowed with a special psychology, being habitually dissatisfied with the fares they chanced to receive. A more generous or extravagant soul would just gracefully jump into a rickshaw and, on reaching his destination, proceed to hand out more than the customary amount. Though the puller would have liked to demand a greater sum in payment, he could not very well do so and perforce had to amble away. A person of another type would pay only the fare, which in his opinion was the correct amount but according to the puller was distinctly deficient. Holding the money already given to him in one outstretched hand and putting on a formidable attitude, the puller would commence a bitter argument. Judging from the frequency with which he indulged in this form of sport, he seemed to relish it and had indeed been specially trained for the purpose. A third type of passenger, conspicuous for cautiousness, would bargain with the puller about the fare and settle this delicate point first, before starting the journey. To this exemplary category, as is to be expected, belonged Lai Pek.

"Twenty cents, and I should say even that is too much," said Lai Pek.

"What!" violently exclaimed the rickshaw man with outraged contempt in his tone. "Do you know how far the theatre is?"

"I am as well aware of the distance as you," said Lai Pek with emphasis. "Take it or leave it."

The puller, who thought he had never come across such a bad customer before, whisked away his rickshaw indignantly, spat on the ground, and grumbled as he went.

After wordy contests with half a dozen pullers, Lai Pek finally secured one who was willing to transport him for thirty cents and, installing himself comfortably in the cushioned vehicle, he proceeded on his journey.

What a harmonious night it was! Innumerable glimmering stars, interspersed at incalculable intervals in the void of infinite space, twinkled so closely together that to the eye they looked as if they were exchanging pleasant secrets in affable conversation. The fair face of the heavens, not deformed by a single straggling cloud, diffused an immense serenity. The life in the streets was not, however, of this description, for all was confusion and tumult as people hurried to and fro, intent on pleasure or business. The shops were brilliantly lighted and maintained a most satisfactory activity.

As befitted a man of sane and sound capacities, Lai Pek displayed no atom of curiosity with regard to such incomprehensible objects as stars; instead, he looked at the many shops, which contained some human interest, eager happiness eloquent on his bland countenance, fully conscious of the important fact that in his possession was one of the choicest concerns in the town.

The rolling rickshaw turned a sharp corner, and the well-proportioned theatre hove in sight. In a shorter time than it takes to tell, Lai Pek was safely deposited outside the building; he paid the carriage fare, over which no further contest ensued, booked a ticket, and entered its inviting portals. He placed himself with dignity in a first-class seat, commanding a glorious view of the stage; an attendant pasted a ticket behind his chair, collected from him the required price, and placed it in a bag slung over his shoulder. The custom of selling tickets for specified classes of seats to spectators before they made their way into the theatre was not in force. An entrance ticket entitled a person only to admittance within the walls; a second slip of paper indicated the seat. If a patron bought only the first, he had the pleasure of witnessing the show on his feet; if he felt tired, he could snatch a short, furtive rest when the ticket seller was in some other part of the hall.

It was still ten minutes before the play was due to commence; Lai Pek looked around him, complacently nodded to a few acquaintances, and seemed well pleased with everything.

A portly man, carrying a walking-stick of proportionate dimensions and wearing what seemed to be a perpetual smile on his face, entered the theatre. Seeing Lai Pek, he made straight for him and gave him a resounding slap on his back, which nearly made Lai Pek jump.

"Fancy finding you here, Lai Pek!" he exclaimed as he seated himself by Lai Pek's side. "What good wind blew you to this place? I haven't seen you for quite a long time. How is business getting on and life in general?"

"So-so," replied Lai Pek. "Nothing unusual has occurred to me; life is just as dull as ever."

"Well, well," said the portly man, whose name was Poh Heow Tu, a rubber dealer by profession, "same here. Nothing ever happens in this monotonous and unenterprising town.

Sometimes it makes one wish that an earthquake would rock the place and give it some vitality," he added facetiously.

Just then a musician stepped upon the stage and blew three loud blasts upon a long trumpet, loud enough to irreparably damage the hearing of a man whose eardrums were unusually fragile. He terminated with a thundering flourish and retired to his seat just in front of the curtain, which separated the stage from the actors' dressing area.

The play commenced with the entry of a man, arrayed in martial accoutrements and possessed of a lengthy beard—the like of which we are not likely to behold nowadays—reaching down to his waist. The entire audience knew immediately that the person who appeared in such glittering splendour was Kuan Yu, the hero of the story—a greater or more valorous hero does not exist in the annals of Chinese history.

In brief, the play depicted one of the most famous scenes from the greatest novel of China, *The Three Kingdoms*. This novel occupies a special place in the affections of the people. It tells of how, when the Han Dynasty of beloved memory came to an inglorious demise at the close of the second century AD and the country became the prey of tyrannical warlords, separated into various divisions, Liu Pei, a descendant of the dynasty, although in poor circumstances, struggled gallantly to keep the flame of his ancestors burning. He and his two inseparable companions, Kuan Yu and Chang Fei, with whom he swore the peach-garden oath of eternal fidelity, and his marvellously resourceful advisor, Chu Ko Liang, underwent strange adventures that never fail to impart a thrill to the reader or spectator.

The episode represented that night dealt with the endeavours of Kuan Yu to escape from the territory under the control of the notorious villain, Tsao Tsao, who had usurped the imperial power and was ambitious to found a new dynasty.

Kuan Yu, who was destined to receive canonization in later ages as Kuan Ti, the God of War, and the two wives of Liu Pei, to whom he was faithful guardian, had fallen into the grasp of the detestable Tsao Tsao. Recognising the matchless bravery of his glorious captive, Tsao Tsao used every means within his power to win Kuan Yu over to his cause and alienate his affections from Liu Pei. But Tsao Tsao's efforts were all in vain. When Kuan Yu received news of the whereabouts of Liu Pei, he, together with the latter's two wives, was determined to journey to Liu Pei's abode. But Tsao Tsao was relectant to let his captive depart, so in order to win his freedom and rejoin his leader, Kuan Yu was forced to vanquish five successive antagonists.

The many deeds re-enacted by Kuan Yu's representative on the stage, played to the clangourous accompaniment of gongs and cymbals, were undeniably gallant and enchanting. The thunder of the performance excited an appropriate degree of enthusiasm in the breasts of the audience.

"That man is an extraordinary actor!" observed the appreciative Lai Pek to his portly friend. "He is giving us a remarkable portrayal of the great Kuan Yu. I have seldom seen anyone play in such a convincing manner."

"Yes," replied Heow Tu, "he is the most brilliant actor in the company, and this troupe is an unusually good one. It has only recently come from China for a tour through Malaya. Everywhere it is meeting with packed houses."

Heow Tu was a regular patron of the theatre, and he liked nothing better than discussions about theatres, actors and actresses, plays, and everything pertaining to them. He was of a jolly disposition and partial to the company of actresses. He had not been tossed and whirled along the river of life by tumultuous torrents but had floated down its course, pleasurably borne along by swaying ripples. His eyes said as much. They were bright, with the sparkling quality of a choice wine; as a matter of fact, this quality might in part have been derived from a copious indulgence in that commodity. He had sowed his wild oats early in youth and to a certain extent still retained his early habits. Contrary to the usual laws of experience, he had retained his prosperity and had not squandered his inheritance; not being so nimble now as he used to be, he had developed greater sobriety in his appearance and a manner of behaviour more in accordance with the proprieties.

"That actress is one of the prettiest imaginable, and her acting is superb! What a clear, flexible voice she possesses!" He turned to Lai Pek with something resembling ecstasy in his mien.

"No doubt she can act," remarked Lai Pek drily. He paid casual visits to the theatre for the sake of the drama, not for the sake of the entangling beauty of actresses. "What a stirring period of activity the end of the Han Dynasty produced," he continued, as if to distract Heow Tu's attention from those bewitching creatures, "but unfortunately it wasn't an activity good for the welfare of the people. It is a strange thing that China should periodically be cursed with lengthy civil wars, as usually occurred between successive dynasties. Heaven must have sent them to punish the viciousness of dynasties after they had endured a considerable length of time and to prepare the way for the foundation of more vigorous ones."

"It always happened that the people suffered the most during the wars. Myriads were killed; their towns were destroyed and their lands devastated. Some of the stories about the sacking of towns make gruesome reading. I wonder why Heaven should have permitted such havoc among the people to punish the evils done by individual emperors," said Heow Tu, who was something of a sceptic in religious matters.

"It is the will of Heaven to do as He does, and we can't penetrate His mysteries," observed Lai Pek fatalistically. "Didn't Confucius teach us not to worry about the secrets of Heaven? I think he was right, just as he was in everything else."

"What surprises me," said Heow Tu, "is that the people were usually very patient under the most terrible calamities. Do you think they loved suffering for its own sake?"

"That is too ridiculous an idea. No man loves pain, however slight, if he can avoid it. What could the people do, however? They couldn't fight against armies. They had to endure their miseries patiently."

For a moment they were absorbed in silent contemplation of the drama on the stage.

"As for that villain, Tsao Tsao," resumed Lai Pek, pointing to the actor who had the misfortune to represent that unattractive character, "I can't conceive how such a monstrous person could possibly have existed. He had no scruples of any sort whatever."

"Indeed, I think he was not so horrible a man as he is depicted. He was a man of literary culture and administrative ability. There have been many villains in Chinese history worse than he. He wasn't the person who started the downfall of the Han Dynasty. Tung Cho, who, as I have no doubt you agree, was perfectly detestable, had preceded him. You know how generously he treated Kuan Yu. I dare say his aim was to win him over to his cause; but still, if he had been a really bad man, he would have put him to death directly when he found he could not succeed in using him."

"I don't agree with you. He was just an artful, diplomatic villain. Have you heard the story of the man who hated Tsao Tsao to such an extent that in his passion he cut off the nose of an actor who was playing his part on the stage? This man was an ardent reader of *The Three Kingdoms,* and he conceived a tremendous aversion towards Tsao Tsao. One day, while he was witnessing a play dealing with that immortal story, he gradually got more and more furious as he beheld the antics of the villain. Finally, he stepped on to the stage and, producing a knife, unexpectedly cut off the nose of the unlucky fellow who was playing Tsao Tsao. When he was arrested and was asked the reason for such extraordinary behaviour, he confessed that he had an uncontrollable antipathy towards the very name of Tsao Tsao, so that as the play progressed, in his fury he identified the actor with the historical personage. As a proof of his attitude of mind, he produced his copy of the book, from which he had burnt out, using incense sticks, every mention of the name Tsao Tsao. I am not going to deny that his conduct was peculiar, but I can understand his feelings," concluded Lai Pek, turning towards his companion with a twinkling eye.

"I am of the opinion that the man was insane. I hope no member of the audience is going to act out in that unpleasant way," said Heow Tu facetiously. "As for these historical plays," he resumed after a pause, "I think they are good; but the scope of drama should be extended by the performance of new plays, like those of the West. We are simply seeing the same old ones over and over again, and this tends to be exceedingly monotonous."

"I think new plays are undesirable," responded Lai Pek. "We have a complete set of stories dealing with the various periods of history, and it's impossible to make really new historical plays. They would still deal with the same material."

"But there is no need for drama to deal with only historical subjects. It can very well concern itself with our modern, everyday life."

"We don't want to come to the theatre to see representations of ordinary life. We can see that in the streets. It would be more sensible to see only scenes far removed from what we usually encounter."

"Stories of ordinary life are not mere records of isolated, everyday incidents. Although they deal with modern people we can recognise as actually existing, they are real tales, constructed with skill, in which separate events follow one another in due order and form a connected whole."

"I can still find no interest whatever in such tame and vulgar stuff. It must be exceedingly boring."

"The interest does not lie only in the story but also in the characterization, wit, humour, and pathos of the piece. And I think it's much better that we don't already know the course of the tale and how its end will come about when we sit down to the play than if we know beforehand exactly how everything is going to happen."

"Well," said Lai Pek, "you may not agree with me, but I consider it fortunate that such plays are not popular among us. If we attend the theatre because we expect to find new stories, we shall very soon come to despise our traditional dramas or they will become unimportant, and we will come to see them only once or twice in comparison with the other sort. That will not be to the good."

Thereupon they lapsed into mutual silence and, save for an occasional remark, their attention was wholly directed to the entertainment before them, which had by this time become exceedingly animated and calculated to make lasting impressions on the audience. The show terminated at midnight.

Lai Pek, on arrival at his house, went to bed, conscious that he had spent a busy and satisfactory day and might now indulge in happy repose.

Chapter 4

Sin Beng Hu's Ménage

At a short distance from the town, by the side of a broad, level highway, which was rendered smooth by a fine coating of tar but which, in consequence, was inclined to be unpleasantly hot under the scorching rays of the noon sun, stood a bungalow of considerable dimensions. Unlike other residences in the vicinity, its position was fixed so that its frontal aspect was turned at an angle of forty-five degrees towards the road. It was encircled by a trim bamboo hedge, and it boasted a garden of orchids and chrysanthemums. Its two-storey brick frame stood with erect dignity, and its blue colour was vastly soothing to the nervous system.

The air pervading the neighbourhood emitted salubrious properties and was of a character calculated to restore spent energies and produce a feeling of robust health. No hypochondriac could escape its benign influence; after half-a-dozen prolonged breaths, he or she would undoubtedly begin to sing and jump for joy. It was no wonder that the birds sang so lustily and melodiously on the rambutan and mangosteen trees, and the gay butterflies and dragonflies swayed gracefully on the fragrant petals.

Several turkeys strutted about, comically jerking their long necks, making gobbling noises, evidently testifying, in their uncouth way, to the glory of their surroundings. A fine flock of white doves sometimes nestled on the roof in the bright sunlight and sometimes, for no perceptible reason whatever, alighted on the ground amid a clatter of wings; these mad capers could only be attributed to a youthful outburst of spirits, materially assisted by the unparalleled beauty of the weather and the exquisite glamour of the scene.

The interior of the house presented a picture of dainty neatness—everything seemed in its proper position. The floor shone; the walls, adorned with paintings of ethereal figures amid beautiful landscapes on silk and scrolls bearing antithetical couplets, created an agreeable impression on the observer. The furniture included a curious blend of Eastern and Western articles, but they were arranged in as harmonious a fashion as possible. The house was, in a word, distinctive and clearly indicated the cultured taste of the owner.

It was ten o'clock in the morning, and the family was assembled in the sitting room, which was finely furnished. Its very appearance—so inviting and cosy—was sufficient to break the bonds of silence and produce and maintain a steady flow of conversation. Total strangers, diffident and tongue-tied, became exuberantly loquacious when they were introduced to this apartment, and they departed from it with a feeling that there was still some hope of their becoming brilliant conversationalists.

Installed in a low stuffed armchair in one corner of the room was Sin Beng Hu, the proud possessor of the house. He was of considerably more than the average height, but this was not compensated for by a proportionate increase in bulk; as a matter of fact he was distinctly inclined to thinness, and his slim build consequently appeared exaggerated. About thirty-one years of age, he looked a bit older, which could be accounted for by his habitual seriousness. However, his deportment could not be described as solemn, for his face was full of animation and his movements alert, while his eyes, fairly shining with persistent optimism, betrayed his enterprising disposition. His whole appearance was neat and bespoke fastidious taste. His hair was neatly parted in the middle and smoothly brushed back; his clothes were spotlessly clean and hung upon him gracefully. Dirt seemed absolutely unable to approach his person, owing, as it were, to a repelling magnetic force between them. He avoided touching anything that was tinged with even a little filth; and, if he did so, through necessity or by accident, he immediately took recourse to soap and water.

He had inherited considerable wealth from his father and had only recently arrived in the town of Lanta. His father, who had engaged in several kinds of commercial enterprise in the course of his life, had bequeathed his property to his three sons, of whom Beng Hu was the youngest. Not much relishing his native town of Gosi and not wishing to compete with his brothers in business, he had left to find a new outlet for his activities. On a previous visit to Lanta several years before, he had been charmed by the place, with its cooler climate and its lakes and hills. He had travelled throughout the length and breadth of Malaya, and he decided that it was more to his taste to make his permanent abode in Lanta. Accordingly, having bought the house that he had chosen, he had it decorated with fastidious care and soon installed himself in it.

Mrs. Sin Beng Hu was seated at a marble table in the centre of the room, and in front of her was a plate of melon seeds, which she was cracking and nibbling with amazing speed. She was young and fair and had no cause to regret her marriage, although it had not begun under happy auspices. She had married for love, in spite of the opposition of her parents, who had other designs for her. Of an impetuous temper, she had conceived romantic notions through the medium of love novels of an extremely sentimental character, which she thought sublime. She attempted to behave in ways she imagined to be captivating; she was always dressed in the latest fashions and made plentiful use of cosmetics. Beyond her poses, however, she possessed a store of good sense, thus rendering her idiosyncrasies mere matters for amusement rather than anger to those around her.

Another occupant of the room was an aunt of Mrs. Sin, who lived with them. Mrs. Pak, whose husband had passed away several years previously, was a childless old lady who had a strong affection for her niece, whom she treated almost like a daughter. She was fussy about trifles and loved nothing better than a good chat about nothing whatever or about the differences that existed between social behaviours from former times and the present day. She did not approve of her niece's flighty ways, but her affection for her made Mrs. Pak tolerate them resignedly.

Mr. and Mrs. Sin were blessed with a son, who at that moment was at school, busily and laboriously scrawling large characters on a slate, and who was petted by his grand-aunt, spoiled by his mother, and treated sternly by his father.

"This is a very nice town," Mrs. Sin was saying with an air of satisfaction. "Although not very exciting, it is extremely agreeable. We have made quite a good number of friends already, and I must say the people here seem pleasant and obliging. Of course, a city would give more pleasures, but all the same, I don't think I shall ever regret having come here."

"The town is tolerable in its way," chimed in Mrs. Pak, "but I rather wish we were still amid our old, familiar surroundings. People find it difficult to separate themselves from what they have been accustomed to all their lives, and I don't blame them for it. Call it sentimentality or what you will, but I am of the opinion that a person should always stick to his native town. As a matter of fact, the majority of people do stay all their lives in some particular town, and I don't know why I should be condemned at my time of life to attempt to fit myself into new surroundings," she concluded woefully.

"There, there, Aunt," said Mrs. Sin playfully, "you make me feel as if I have committed an atrocious crime whenever you talk like that. Really and truly, you must confess that your health has been declining for the last few years, and you used to charge it to the bad climate of Gosi, the heat of which produced in you a feeling of weariness, as well as headache. I haven't heard you complain of those ills at all since we came here."

"You are talking nonsense, Sui Chu," retorted Mrs. Pak. "It's true I don't feel so headachy now, but I think that it is just a temporary phase because I have had so many other things to occupy my mind lately that I haven't had time to think of my health. Besides, even if the climate here is more beneficial, still that and a few other advantages cannot compensate for the many disadvantages I have incurred by leaving Gosi. But, of course, it's no use trying to drive sense into a scatterbrained girl like you; you will never understand my reasons. You have never understood anything I said," she concluded, resigned.

Mrs. Sin laughed but did not pursue that particular discussion further, as she well knew that contradictions only served to increase her aunt's obstinate adherence to her opinions and would soon produce from her a moral lecture.

"This place should offer a good scope for commercial enterprise," remarked Beng Hu, as he turned a cigarette between his fingers and thumped it thrice on a matchbox, preparatory to lighting it. "It is rather a sleepy town, and there is hardly any merchant here who has a sense of modern business methods. Their customers come to them by chance, and there is nothing attractive about their shops, nothing that can tempt anyone to take a careful look around. People should be made to open their purses as liberally as possible, and they are not likely to do so unless the goods are bound to catch their fancy so that they are loath to do without them. Yes, this town is the right place for new enterprise," he repeated with evident conviction, talking half to himself.

"I think you are right," agreed his wife. "What definite plans have you formed for launching the business?"

"It's as well to begin as early as possible. Today is the twenty-first; we will open our firm on the first day of next month. I have already rented the premises in Pee Ka Street, which forms the busiest section of the town. Most of the necessary employees have been engaged and told to report for duty on the stated day. As a good deal of business success depends on the conduct of the salesmen, I have selected them with particular care. It is astonishing how few people in this place are acquainted with the proper methods of approaching the prospective buyer. Most of the people who were interviewed by me were quite ignorant of the most elementary essentials of salesmanship."

"What are the characteristics of good salesmanship, as you call it?" inquired Mrs. Pak, displaying an air of deep interest.

"Well, the test is the ability to induce people to buy what you have to sell. A good salesman can even make someone buy things he does not really want," explained Beng Hu.

"That is extremely curious," said Mrs. Pak with an expression of incredulity. "How could a person buy things he doesn't want, unless he is a good-for-nothing spendthrift?"

"What I meant was that a person could be persuaded to purchase something that he originally did not intend to have; owing to the eloquence of the salesman, however, he changes his mind about its desirability. He buys it because he is tempted by it," replied Beng Hu.

"I can't believe that anybody is clever enough to do that—not with me, anyhow," she said with decided conviction. "Before I enter a shop, I have concluded beforehand what particular article I want and what qualities such an article should possess. If I find what suits me, I buy it; if it does not come up to my expectations, I go to another shop. I am sure no salesman can make me believe that a potato is an apple," she concluded triumphantly.

"No one would expect you to believe such a thing, Aunt," laughed Mrs. Sin. Then, turning to her husband, she asked, "What name do you propose to give our shop? It should bear some propitious meaning, of course."

"Oh, that is easily settled," he replied, waving his hand gracefully. "I don't attach much importance to mere names. Anything will do for me. But for the sake of some distinctive title, what do you say to this: Fleet Horse? May our business reach prosperity as swiftly as a fleet horse reaches its goal!"

"That is quite suitable," said Mrs. Sin.

"Our firm will deal in general merchandise," continued Beng Hu. "We will gradually try to increase the variety of goods in stock, so that in the course of time people will be able to buy everything there, from stationery to clothing, from fruit to gramophone records. In fact, I intend to make it the principal firm in the town," he added, with an expression of considerable importance.

Just then their conversation was interrupted by the entrance of two visitors, Mr. and Mrs. Tee Tow Lia, whom they proceeded to welcome effusively. Tow Lia, a cloth merchant by profession, was blessed with a short figure of remarkable rotundity; his clothes fit tightly upon him. His gait was ungainly in the extreme, his head rested upon a thick neck and he possessed a double chin. He was really interested only in trifles, but his air of portentous solemnity gave the impression that whatever he did or said was extremely important. His wife, aged about twenty-seven, was neither beautiful nor ugly, neither stout nor thin. She was endowed with an equally frivolous disposition, but her appearance was not touched by any speck of heaviness. It was inconceivable that she found anything serious in existence, and her tongue continually produced a tinkling flow of chatter, expressing whatever came uppermost in her mind. Like many other loquacious people, she laboured under the delusion that her conversation was exceptionally entertaining and that she was helping to while away the tedium of her audience.

"It is very kind of you to pay us a visit, Mrs. Tee," said Mrs. Sin, her tone expressing the deepest gratitude. "How is your little daughter getting on? I hope she has recovered from her recent illness."

"She is almost completely recovered, except for a slight cough," replied Mrs. Tee. "Thank you for your inquiry. I hope our town is agreeable to you and that you will appreciate it more and more as time goes on. I must confess that I am of the opinion that, though it is not bad, a city is much better. We are tied down to this place by business."

"Oh, it is lovely!" exclaimed Mrs. Sin rapturously. "I already feel as if I have been intimate with it from my birth, and all my happiness is wound up with it. It was a lucky day that we came here," she added gracefully.

"Indeed," said Mrs. Tee; "I am glad that you are pleased with it. You will soon come to know all the people here, and you will find some of them are pleasant to associate with." She shook her head playfully, with a smile that indicated her awareness that she was one of the most pleasant of the pleasant creatures in that town.

While this delightful conversation passed between their respective spouses, the two men were silent listeners. Mrs. Sin invited Mrs. Tee to take a walk with her in the garden to pick some flowers, and they went out. Mrs. Pak suddenly recollected that she had to make certain purchases, which she did not specifically mention, and likewise left the room.

"I remember you told me that you were going to establish a firm in this place," began Tow Lia. "I hope your arrangements are near completion."

"Oh yes," was the response. "I have definitely made arrangements for the shop to open at the beginning of next month."

"I trust your business will be very prosperous," said Tow Lia. "If I could be of any assistance to you, please don't hesitate to ask me. Whatever help I can render you will only make me happy."

"Thank you very much indeed for your kind words. To tell the truth, your advice would be invaluable, and I shall avail myself freely of it without any ceremony," smiled Beng Hu to the highly delighted Tow Lia. "To begin with, would you mind telling me the prevailing state of business in this town?"

"With the greatest pleasure," answered the other gravely. "We are having a run of prosperity—I might even say remarkable prosperity. This is in evidence everywhere; the shops teem with people. Of course, this is just a reflection of the general prosperity of the country, the prices of its staple products, rubber and tin, being at maximum. There is no indication of any unfavourable turn of affairs. Most kinds of business activity are represented here. There is keen competition, but I for one don't mind that, as it makes life so much more interesting," he added with unbending seriousness.

"What is the general character of the merchants?" asked Beng Hu. "I hope you will excuse my asking such a question, but I should like to know how to conduct myself towards them."

"They are for the most part sufficiently honest and just in their dealings," said Tow Lia. "Of course, that doesn't mean that one can trust any particular man completely. He may be an exception or he may deviate from his customary upright path under certain circumstances. The best policy is to be fair in one's dealings but not to place too much trust in people. I have seen some respectable and reputedly honest men turn into rogues. The persons here are also polite. Unfortunately, many of them are rather stingy and hard to deal with, obstinately clinging to certain preconceived notions. Such people dislike new suggestions. We have a club here," he continued in a voice replete with intense interest, "a club reserved exclusively for businessmen. I will introduce you to it as soon as you wish. You will quickly come to know more about the nature of the people there than anything I can tell you."

"Whereabouts is this club?" asked Beng Hu.

"Leh Haw Street, at the eastern end of the town," replied Tow Lia. "It is a secluded spot, and most of us often gather there till late at night. Do you play mahjong? It is rather a popular form of recreation with us."

"Oh yes, I like an occasional game," replied Beng Hu.

"That's excellent!" exclaimed Tow Lia. "It's the best of all games of chance. The stakes are not high, and people don't get ruined by it as they may by other kinds of gambling. The sounds caused by the pieces striking the table are quite pleasant to hear. Really, I pity the man who does not like it," he concluded in a condescendingly sympathetic manner.

"How many members are there?" asked Beng Hu.

"About seventy," replied Tow Lia. "Among them you will discover different types of characters. Some are very industrious and have their whole being wrapped up in their business. They seem to regard the club as a place where they can assemble and discuss business at night. A few people, very few, I am happy to state, are strange to the point of being eccentric. But as I find that they are harmless, I do not mind their nonsense so much. On the whole, the members are a pleasant lot, and you will find the club an excellent place. I go there regularly," he concluded complacently.

While this important discussion was going on, Mrs. Sin and Mrs. Tee were walking about the garden and holding a conversation, scarcely less useful and much more interesting. Each of them was holding in her hand a bunch of flowers, freshly severed from their stalks, dedicated to a higher destiny than dying an inglorious death on their native supports, withered and ugly. Alas,

Full many a flower is born to blush unseen
And waste its sweetness on the desert air

But, like so many lucky individuals, these particular flowers, endowed with no distinguished merits whatsoever but those owed solely to the whims of tyrannous fortune, escaped such a melancholy end. The purpose of their existence was to adorn the table or—wonder of wonders!—the exquisite feminine person. Who could deny that theirs was a fate to be envied!

"Of course, life is apt to be monotonous here," Mrs. Tee was saying. "There is little to do and hardly any variety in the way of entertainment. The days follow one another in regular succession and pass by without leaving any significant impression on one's memory. I would have much preferred a continual series of exciting days. They say excitement may fray one's nerves, but I don't believe a word of it. I tried to persuade my husband many times to move to some city, but unluckily he is tied down by business. So I do the next best thing. Periodically, I spend many weeks in Singapore. You must have visited it, I suppose," she added.

"Yes, but only twice so far," smiled Mrs. Sin.

"I shall be going there again in about a month's time. I shall be very glad if you could come along with me."

"Well, I really wish I could," replied Mrs. Sin. "I must think it over first."

After a most amiable conversation on a comprehensive variety of topics, ranging from clothes to cookery, they re-entered the house together, and soon afterwards Mr. and Mrs. Tee took their departure, in an atmosphere of the utmost friendliness and amid polite expressions.

Chapter 5

The Rubber Estate

"Of all the vexations that I have ever encountered," remarked Lai Pek to Hwey Pin, as they stood disconsolately on a patch of grass by the side of the rough, stony road, watching the driver as he bent over the tyre, endeavouring to locate the puncture, "this is the sort that fills me with the most impatience. To be proceeding smoothly towards the end of one's journey, and then to feel a sudden bump and hear a loud explosion, followed by an interval of waiting—what an irritating circumstance! It is not exactly cool today, either, and here we are, standing underneath the broiling rays of the sun."

Hwey Pin, who was following the movements of the sweating driver with the maximum amount of interest, as he was just as anxious to resume the ride with the minimum amount of delay, smiled a faint, sympathetic smile. He was escorting Lai Pek to the rubber estate he recommended, and he wanted him to receive a favourable impression of its worth as soon as possible so that the transaction might have a speedy termination and he could feel the commission jingling in his pocket.

At last, to their intense relief, the car was put in a fit state to continue again; they proceeded along smoothly without encountering any further misadventure. They rushed past stretches of shimmering green paddy fields, their long stalks waving in rhythmic motion, and vegetable gardens where toil-worn figures moved wearily yet steadfastly from row to row, digging, weeding, and manuring. At scattered intervals, they observed women or boys with cheerful countenances sitting on the grass by turbid ponds or brooks, fishing rods in their hands. Occasionally, merry groups of women, workers in the tin mines in the vicinity, dressed in black blouses and wearing big red kerchiefs over their heads, sauntered along and were soon swallowed up in the distance. Many a village, with a solitary street and its collection of sundry goods shops, was traversed; many a kampong flashed past with its attap huts standing on stilts that were to all appearances very fragile, looking as if they would give way at any time but which, nevertheless, had supported their square structures with whole families inside them for an untold length of time. After winding through a twisting, steep section of the road, they finally arrived at the village of Chola, which lay in sleepy reverie at the foot of a hill covered with dense forest, green and glamorous in the distance.

The village, situated a goodly distance from a town of any size, occupied a position of some importance, which was increasing yearly. It boasted three tarred streets, perfectly parallel to one another; a market with a floor of concrete and a tiled roof; a school; and a railway station, at which even mail trains condescended to pause. There happened to be a fair that day, and all the Malays from the surrounding kampongs who had anything to sell were gathered together to display their wares, which were of their own production: jack-fruit, durians, pineapples, blachan, chillis, green vegetables, tapioca, and basket work. They sat on the ground by the side of the road, having installed themselves there from the earliest peep of dawn. Loud was the din and merry were the purchasers, ambling leisurely from seller to seller and bargaining with infinite volubility, pretending to disparage what they really appreciated and yearned to possess. The food vendors were especially popular: seated on low stools, with two baskets or stalls on either side to hold the ingredients, they cooked and served without a pause. There was a satay man, roasting pieces of beef held on sticks about six inches long made from the branches of coconut trees; by his side squatted an individual frying bananas dipped in flour; a little farther along was a retailer of laksa, the white rolls of vermicelli gleaming in their bowls of hot, spicy soup.

Lai Pek and his companions stared at the scene with immense interest as they slowly wended their way through the crowd. They stopped on a solitary road some distance beyond the limits of the village, bounded on both sides by rows and rows of rubber trees. Leaving the car behind, they walked along a narrow path for about a quarter of an hour before they reached the estate, which was the object of their excursion.

It was situated on hilly ground, flanked by a dense jungle; the red earth was strewn with withered leaves and brown seeds whose shells, cracking under the heels, revealed a yellowish pulp. An eerie, oppressive atmosphere brooded over the dark expanse of land, wrapped in a mantle of gloom, suffused with silent mystery. The trees, planted in a regular chequered pattern, rose erect; a few feet above the ground their tall, smooth trunks bore the grooves of artistic carvings, from which daily flowed milky latex, to be coagulated into marketable rubber, around whose strange fluctuation in prices had revolved the economic prosperity of the tropical peninsula. An occasional squirrel scampered along the branches, enjoying its freedom amid congenial surroundings. A brook, with tiny fish winding in and out of its numerous cavities, flowed over a bed of white stones, betraying on its surface just a trace of the turbidity and wildness suggestive of its jungle origin and its recent, perilous descent down a steep precipice.

Lai Pek went up to the trees and scrutinised the trunks carefully, endeavouring to thoroughly examine the nature of the bark and the way it had undergone the process of tapping. He was evidently not at all dissatisfied with the results of his profound research for, turning to Hwey Pin, he remarked, "The trees are in good condition. The tapping has not been done with negligence—that is, as far as I can see. The rest of the estate is planted with mature trees like these, I suppose?"

"Oh yes," replied Hwey Pin in a satisfied tone. "We'll take a walk around and view the estate as thoroughly as possible. In the meantime, we had better go to the huts of the tappers and the buildings where the rubber is treated and smoked. They are somewhere in the middle of the land, and we'll reach them in a short time."

"That is an excellent idea," said Lai Pek. "We can take a rest in the huts before we make any further surveys."

With that they proceeded along at a nimble pace and soon reached an open plot of ground, on which stood a collection of flimsy attap houses, with their sloping brown roofs and wooden walls, between whose planks penetrated the greater proportion of the light the interiors received. The floors, made of black earth pounded into a hard, compact mass, were uneven in places and contained good-sized pools of muddy water. Rising only a few feet above the ground, they were enclosed by tall fruit trees: coconut palms, with deep grooves cut into their sides to render climbing easier, and durian trees, with their drab trunks and branches, loaded with round, thorny fruit, about the size of a man's head, some of which were still green. Some had changed to a mellow yellowish hue, ready to drop with perpendicular force on unwary passers-by; they had been known to knock the faculties out of a man and lay him flat on his back. Evidently, durian felt a profound aversion towards being rudely and unceremoniously plucked from their perches. The man who yearned for the sweet taste and pungent, peculiar smell of their golden, tender pulp had to wait patiently a few feet away until a premonitory crack was audible; then, a minute later, a spiky ball would descend with a thump to the ground. Mango trees drooped their branches in all directions; green banana groves occupied a respectable corner, and around their bases gambolled a brood of chickens.

The overseer of the estate, a man inured to hardships, with a wiry form and a countenance wrinkled and tanned but cheerful and patient, content with his wife and children and regular meals, extended a hearty welcome to the two visitors and invited them into his hut, where they were soon regaled with a pot of hot tea. Unending toil had been his lot from early boyhood, before his departure from his ancestral home in China, where he tended the cows and tilled the fields from faint dawn to gloomy dusk. After he landed in Malaya, a bewildered immigrant, he was quick to adapt himself to changed conditions and willing to perform any task, however arduous and unpalatable. He had worked in the tin mines and lost a finger when his left hand got caught in the wheel of a dredge. He had felled trees in the mangrove swamps that were infested with anopheles mosquitoes, which injected malarial parasites into the victims they bit, and gray, scaly crocodiles and marauding tigers from the depths of the jungle. In his youth, his ambition had been to make a fortune so that he might return in triumph to his native village and erect a stately structure as a monument to the family name. His dream had evaporated, but his regrets were not tinged with any discontent, and his temper remained unsoured through his catalogue of misfortunes and abortive attempts at wealth, in spite of the fact that some of his fellow immigrants had achieved what he had failed to do, through no fault of his own.

After a short spell of conversation, in which Lai Pek obtained from the overseer some information of an interesting character, the three men proceeded on a tour of inspection of the rubber production plant and the part of the estate adjacent to the forest. They first arrived at a building where the latex was treated. In one corner of the concrete floor was a deep well, its square sides lined with bricks; a few feet of water bubbled through the white sand that formed its bed. The clear juice was collected in oval clay tanks and, mixed with acid, was left to curdle in shallow trays. The coarse sheets that formed were first pressed between smooth rollers and then beautified by being passed through cylindrical iron rollers, on which was engraved a pattern of chequered lines. In the smoke room, which occupied a shed a short distance apart from other houses, the sheets were subjected to heat and gradually assumed a clear brown hue. They were then placed in stacks, ready for transportation to the rubber dealers in the nearest town.

When Lai Pek, Hwey Pin and the overseer arrived at the fringe of the forest, they were greeted by some large and small monkeys, which looked down curiously at them from their lofty seats on thick branches and chattered volubly among themselves. The forest did not bear a particularly inviting appearance, and Lai Pek never dreamed of violating its boundaries and exploring its hidden treasures of fauna and flora. A green snake rapidly glided past them and lost itself among the thick layer of putrefying leaves that cloaked the earth. Suddenly, Hwey Pin uttered a suppressed oath, and the next moment he was tugging at a bloated leech that was enjoying a hearty meal on his leg. He threw it away with a curse, and the overseer quickly extracted a pinch of tobacco from his pouch to stop the bleeding.

After securing all the knowledge he wanted concerning the estate, Lai Pek departed with Hwey Pin for home, well satisfied with his trip. A short time later, he became the proud proprietor of that piece of land. He was greatly gratified by its acquisition, and his satisfaction with life was enormously enhanced.

Chapter 6

The Launching of a Business Enterprise

At last, the great day of the formal inauguration of the business planned by Beng Hu arrived. The final touches had been given to all the necessary preparations. The employees were all duly engaged, the premises piled high with a glittering stock of new goods, and the attention of the public sufficiently attracted by advertisements in the local paper and by the lavish distribution of handbills. Several days before, a boy could be observed trudging from house to house, busily depositing large sheets of green paper on window sills or placing them in the hands of people who happened to be standing near their doors; he seemed to possess an inexhaustible supply. The curious observer, on looking at one of these sheets, would be confronted with an announcement to the effect that a new firm, bearing the picturesque name *Fleet Horse,* was about to commence its career, with specifications as to the place and date thereof. His attention would be called to the fact that the firm arose in order to meet a real demand and that integrity, prompt service, and bargain prices were its fundamental principles. The patronage of the public was earnestly solicited, and the bill concluded with the important news that for a week, commencing from the first of next month, there would be a sale, and everyone was cordially invited to take advantage of this offer, an offer which he or she was seldom likely to encounter.

A more favourable morning could not be imagined. The sky was clear and undefiled by masses of dark clouds that might elect at any time to liberate doses of unwelcome rain. The sun, well-awakened from its nocturnal sleep, began to generously distribute its abundant energy, on which depends the subsistence of the world. It is no wonder that in all systems of mythology the god of the sun is a principal deity and that the ancient Persians worshipped him on mountain tops.

But to Beng Hu, as he awoke on that memorable dawn and looked up at the sky with casual scrutiny, the sun did not appear as a divine personage but as the herald of another day, the source of the light essential to work. After having stretched his arms and legs to such a considerable extent that they were in danger of imminent dislocation, he sprang out of bed with a most uncommonly agile bound. After having performed the requisite ablutions of refined civilization, he sat down to breakfast. Mrs. Sin had not yet awakened, so he was left alone to his meal, a substantial one indeed, which, however, he ate abstractedly, as his mind was temporarily occupied with more important details, giving him an incapacity to concentrate on the mere process of eating.

After a short rest at the conclusion of his meal, he left the house in his car. The streets had begun to stir with life, having shaken off the previous night's lethargy. On his way he passed the market, which was thronged with buyers. Many clerks were proceeding to their offices on bicycles, looking as if they wished that it were a holiday and that they could pass their time in their clubs playing billiards. The car soon came to a stop in Pee Ka Street, and Beng Hu alighted outside his shop.

It had just been opened by the chief clerk, who was acting in the capacity of general superintendent and in control of operations. All the employees, numbering more than a dozen, including salesmen and coolies, were already assembled, and they looked as smart as the furniture. Being strangers to one another, they by no means felt very much at ease.

The shop comprised two houses, the partition between which had been knocked down so that its width was about equal to its length. It occupied an advantageous position, being situated at the junction of the two busiest streets, and it was open on two sides. Its outer aspect was imposing; on the wall, painted in Chinese characters a foot high, were the two glorious words FLEET HORSE. It bore a new coat of brown paint and looked perfectly clean and untarnished.

Immediately after his arrival, Beng Hu ordered crackers to be fired and, as they were of a type that exploded with impressive loudness, the rapid succession of sounds was highly enlivening. This announced the official opening of the establishment, and soon the shop was thronged with a most gratifying array of purchasers, or at least spectators, who inspected everything with evident curiosity.

A splendid maze saluted the eyes of everyone who passed the threshold. What a glittering array of goods there was! The stock, which was divided into different categories, was extensive and varied. The articles were neatly arranged in glass cases, and attached to each was a cardboard label, indicating the regular price, as well as the generously discounted price in force during the grand sale. One could purchase all household requirements there: it was indeed an impressive shop.

In one case were all the necessary toilet items, from perfume to powder—exquisite substances with an irresistible appeal to feminine hearts. In an adjacent case were arranged other more mundane articles that, perhaps, served more useful purposes—toothbrushes, toothpaste, combs, scissors, etc. Other cases exhibited cloth, shoes, socks of all colours, and hats of all shapes. Culinary utensils sprawled in profusion; electric cookers and refrigerators were visible. Toys and dolls were not overlooked but, on the contrary, occupied a respectable corner. Even fresh fruits, both those grown locally and those imported from abroad, displayed their gleaming glory. Only a cantankerous dyspeptic could have failed to discover anything suitable to his needs amid such luxuriant variety.

As the morning advanced, the heat grew more uncomfortable in quality, but the customers more comfortable in quantity—the employees perspired freely from both causes, though. As it was their first day of work, their alertness showed no diminution. They amply fulfilled the slogan of thc firm, which was inserted in the local paper and even flashed across the screen in the local movie theatre: *prompt and cheerful service guaranteed.* It is hard to say from what source of inspiration they derived their cheerfulness, but cheerful they began and cheerful they remained.

"If our present volume of sales could be steadily maintained, we should have nothing to fear for the future. Our shop will be the emporium of the town," remarked Beng Hu to the chief clerk towards the end of the day.

"I am sure it will attain that position very soon," said the clerk, with an emphatic note of conviction in his smooth voice. He was a man whose business acumen, derived from a long clerical experience in commercial firms, was indubitable. Consequently, his opinion afforded the highest gratification to his employer. The sun had now nearly completed its daily journey across the sky and, in spite of his abundant vitality, Beng Hu was glad to don his coat, ready for departure.

"There is no appetizer like a worthy day's work," thought he as he drove home, his brain still revolving over the events of the day with maximum pleasure.

After dinner, which he ate approximately one hour after the sun went down, Beng Hu departed for the club, to which he had been introduced by Tee Tow Lia. It occupied a detached building at one end of the town, and its bright lights were conspicuous amid its gloomy environs. As Beng Hu pushed open the folding doors, loud laughter from a group of mahjong players, evidently in the very highest state of enthusiasm, filled the room. He beheld Tow Lia among them, vigorously striking the pieces against the table, his face immobile but his eyes dancing with excitement, oblivious to his surroundings.

"Here is Mr. Sin," said Poh Heow Tu, looking up with a smile at Sin Beng Hu. "Congratulations on the successful opening of your business, Mr. Sin. Never have I seen such a glorious throng of people gathered in a shop on its first day in this town—never! Your enterprise will prove a tremendous success; that is a foregone conclusion."

"Thank you, Mr. Poh," replied Beng Hu with a self-depreciatory smile, "you are very kind. My business does not deserve your excessive praises."

"Coming for relaxation, eh?" exclaimed Tow Lia. "You can take my place after this game is over, if you like."

"Thanks, but I can't very well inconvenience you," said Beng Hu.

"Oh, you can have my place," offered another player. "I want to go home." He was one of those who act on the maxim that it is not wise to tempt Fortune beyond her endurance but better to be content with a modest portion of her bounties—he had been winning till then, and he was extremely anxious to take his departure.

Lee Lai Pek was seated near the table, watching the game; he was on one of his rare visits, instigated chiefly by the desire not to fall absolutely out of contact with his fellows in social life. He scanned Beng Hu with immense curiosity, for he recognised him as the distinguished stranger who had made the striking amount of purchases at his shop about ten days before.

"Let me introduce you to Mr. Lee Lai Pek," said Tow Lia to Beng Hu. "Mr. Lee does not often frequent the club, as he has more worthy matters to occupy him."

Lai Pek and Beng Hu both laughed heartily and bowed to each other in orthodox fashion.

"I think I have had the honour of meeting Mr. Sin before," said Lai Pek. "He was once a customer of mine, and a very good customer too."

Here they laughed again with great gusto. Beng Hu seated himself in the chair that the successful player had vacated, and a fresh game was commenced, the participants showing renewed enthusiasm, which made Lai Pek follow its intricacies with equal fascination. Beng Hu, with erect deportment and dignified mien, played his pieces with cautious, deliberate foresight. Tow Lia was imbued with a distinct inclination towards the reckless and, endeavouring to score great victories, he lost heavily. The jovial Heow Tu maintained an imperturbable temper whether he won or lost and laughed on every possible occasion, calling for a drink now and then. The remaining member of the quartet—whose eyes, set in a face expressing the greatest miserliness, possessed the remarkable property of winking many times in rapid succession at intervals of almost imperceptible duration, so that they appeared to be twitching continuously—played so slowly that it sometimes exasperated the others beyond endurance. Tow Lia remonstrated with him several times, remarking that at the rate they were progressing, the play, instead of being a thing of pleasure, was becoming a burden. But his observations were unheeded, and Tow Lia almost lost his temper, which was sharpened by his accumulated losses.

"What induced you to establish a business in this little town, Mr. Sin?" asked Heow Tu, by way of conversation. "With your capital and organizing ability, you could embark on some more enterprising venture in a city and increase your wealth enormously. I can't imagine success running away from you."

"You have too high an opinion of my worth," replied Beng Hu. "People say 'the ring should fit the finger'. I sincerely don't think I can achieve any outstanding success in the fierce competition of a big city. In any case, I am not much concerned with wealth. Business is interesting, but it is a secondary thing with me—I do not want to spend my time in idleness, and I like to be of service to my fellow men. I think that if extortionate profits are not made, business is a real instrument for promoting the welfare of a community."

"You possess a noble soul," exclaimed Heow Tu enthusiastically, "and I entirely agree with you."

Lai Pek was struck dumb with amazement as Beng Hu proceeded, and he wondered whether the latter could be making a true exposition of his views or whether he had some deep design in uttering such obvious absurdities, which no man in his senses could possibly subscribe to and which only a person deficient in taste would attempt to pass off as jokes. He could not believe, under the most persuasive eloquence, that a man could have no desire for the further increase of his riches and that he could regard commerce as an occasion for the display of pedantic benevolence. He earnestly scanned Beng Hu's face for a lurking trace of some ulterior intent, but he was thwarted by the search. *He must be a mental defective,* he thought. His former high opinion of Beng Hu dropped down a precipice with frightful rapidity, danced for a wild instant in the vortex below, and disappeared beneath its fury. The young man, whom he had formerly imagined to be a remarkable person, was after all a nincompoop. Lai Pek was immensely relieved to discover this, for although he did not like to admit the thought into his consciousness, he had begun to entertain a secret fear that he had encountered a formidable rival who would make his position precarious. His superb confidence, after a slight tilt, was completely restored to its normal state of equilibrium.

"I came to this place chiefly because of its beauty and pleasant climate," Beng Hu was saying as he stuck his thirteen pieces on their ends and arranged them in a row before him.

"I feel that I can cultivate a more pleasurable mode of life here than in a city."

"Indeed!" commented Lai Pek. "What is your ideal of a satisfactory life—the ideal that you pursue?"

"I have not exactly formed an ideal," said Beng Hu with a smile. "I love a reasonable amount of tranquillity and leisure—not too excessive, of course. Beautiful scenery is one of the elements of happiness. I love lakes and woods."

"Lakes and woods!" exclaimed Lai Pek incredulously. "Please, Mr. Sin, tell me what kind of pleasure you find in them. I never knew before that any person could enjoy them." There was just a hint of sarcasm in his voice, marring his habitual politeness—he had to chain with shackles of iron an ardent desire to roar with amusement at such nonsense. Never in all his extensive experience had he encountered a man endowed with so fantastic a temperament, although he had run full tilt against many curious eccentrics at one time or another.

"The same sort of pleasure one finds in all forms of beauty," replied Beng Hu serenely. Had he been aware of the odd impression he was making, his inner tranquility may well have suffered a rude jolt, like that of an electric shock. "They charm in the same way as jade and curios. I can spend whole hours revelling in their glories. Don't you love them, Mr. Poh?"

"Oh, I love beauty indeed," said Heow Tu with a sly smile. "But I must confess I haven't taken an interest in that branch. Nature is too poetic for me, too sublime."

"I should say that Nature is very dull," affirmed Lai Pek with noticeable emphasis.

The clock sounded its maximum number of strokes with inexorable distinctness, indicating its displeasure at the continuing presence of humanity in its vicinity. The members of the club took the hint and precipitately departed to recuperate for the morrow. Tow Lia was in a state of profound chagrin at the depletion of his purse; Heow Tu was in a corresponding state of exultation from the opposite cause and looked fatter and jollier than ever as he hummed a tune all the way home. Lai Pek and Beng Hu separated with expressions of mutual esteem on the pavement, and the hearty smile that lit the face of the former had a different origin from that deducible from his words.

Chapter 7

Smitten

The whole family was at breakfast. It was a holiday; therefore nobody was in a hurry. Sum Goh, who, as a teacher, was conscientious in his work and paid great attention to his pupils, was pondering over the welfare of a boy whom he liked for his diligent attention to his studies and his good behaviour. He wondered what had befallen the boy, who had been absent from school for several days.

In the course of casual conversation, Sum Goh mentioned that he was thinking of paying a visit to the house of his pupil to find out what had happened to him.

"Who is his father?" asked Lai Pek.

"Low Tua Sai," replied Sum Goh.

"Oh!" interjected Lai Pek. "That reminds me. I have been rather remiss in keeping contact with my friends. I have known Low Tua Sai for a number of years, but I have not seen him for quite some time. What do you say if we all go together?"

Mrs. Lee was agreeable. She was acquainted with Mrs. Low, and she was always ready for a good chat.

"Yes," she said, "a courtesy call on our part is appropriate."

Sum Goh raised no objection, and so it came about that not long thereafter they sallied forth. They soon reached their destination. Their car drove slowly up a lane of red earth and stopped before a brown bungalow. They received a hearty welcome from the family, and all were soon comfortably seated in the drawing-room.

Sum Goh inquired about his pupil. It transpired that he had been stricken with fever, but he was now almost recovered and would be able to attend school in a couple of days' time. Low Tua Sai explained that he would give the boy a letter on the day of his return to school requesting that his absence be excused. He was gratified at his guest's evident interest in his son, and he praised him for his abilities as a teacher and his goodness as a man, so much so that the poor fellow was hugely embarrassed.

To relieve his discomfort, Sum Goh gazed first at some pictures of boats, flowers, phoenixes, and unicorns that ornamented the walls and then at his highly polished shoes. There was an excellent painting of the Eight Immortals, in whom were enshrined various conceptions of happiness, taking a journey across the sea by a most peculiar method of locomotion. They shone with extreme merriment, each sitting on a separate article, like a sword, or a basket, or some fantastic marine animal.

Sum Goh was scanning this picture with admiration when a young woman entered who had evidently just been spending her time in the garden, as she was carrying a bunch of gardenias. She was not more than nineteen years of age, and possessed a face of unusual beauty and charm. Her dark, lustrous hair harmonized with her dark, sparkling eyes, which shone with an intense interest in life, coupled with innocent frankness. She was naturally happy, as her shining smile revealed. Her dress, a long gown of pale green silk, closely fitting, outlined her dainty figure to advantage. She walked with a lofty, erect carriage, the gracefulness of her gait enhanced by a slightly swaying motion.

Sum Goh stared at this vision so long and with such a concentrated gaze that she blushed, and he quickly fixed his eyes on the same enchanting picture that had attracted his attention before her entry, his face in turn aflame with acute discomfort. She advanced slowly and addressed Mrs. Lee with such entrancing modesty that that lady fairly beamed with gratified smiles.

"What flowers have you plucked this morning, Gek Kim?" asked her mother. "Show them to Mrs. Lee."

"Oh! They are marvellous!" exclaimed Mrs. Lee rapturously. "You possess wonderful taste, Gek Kim."

"She is very fond of flowers," explained Mrs. Low. "She spends a good deal of time every morning in the garden, going from plant to plant, inspecting them as a gardener. I can't understand this passion at all. Flowers are lovely in their way, and I suppose all women love them, but I certainly don't like to look at plants for more than a few minutes at a time."

"I think it's pretty interesting to pass one's time in a garden. One gets the benefit of fresh air also," said Sum Goh, summoning up the courage to put forth this remarkable utterance.

"These young people nowadays have got such strange ideas," said Low Tua Sai, rubbing his spectacles and placing them on the very tip of his broad nose. He was a little, wizened man with an easygoing disposition, indulgent to his family—especially his daughter—and very generous to all who had the fortune to come in contact with him.

Sum Goh and Gek Kim exchanged a mutual smile at her father's remark. Her radiant happiness was indescribable, and under the charm of her easy manners, Sum Goh gradually lost all his diffidence.

"And of all the absurd things she does—one that I have in vain attempted to dissuade her from doing—she paints, wasting energy on pure nonsense," said her mother.

"What a wonderful person you are, Miss Low!" exclaimed Sum Goh. "Please tell me what pictures you draw."

"Oh, they are just trifling sketches in water colour," smiled Gek Kim, "not worth mentioning."

"I have a great desire to see them," said Sum Goh. "Would you kindly show me your collection?"

"With the greatest pleasure," replied Gek Kim, "but I am afraid you will only feel great disappointment on seeing them."

She skipped upstairs, and in a few moments she returned with an album under her arm. It contained some pleasant watercolour paintings and pen sketches of idealized natural scenes, executed with some grace, well illustrating her sanguine temperament. The company were loud in their praises, especially Mrs. Lee, who held up for special admiration a sketch depicting a flock of swallows wheeling above a green field after a refreshing rain shower.

"Perfectly marvellous!" exclaimed Mrs. Lee. "If I were to hold a brush in my hand for a hundred years, I would still be unable to draw even the tail of a swallow." She laughed heartily, evidently at the very height of humour.

"This is a very charming little scene," remarked Sum Goh, extracting from the album a sheet with a pond painted on it and a brood of ducklings swimming gaily, two of them in the act of diving. "Does this represent a real pond, Miss Low?"

“The pond is in one corner of our garden at the back,” smiled Gek Kim. “It is a very small one, though.”

“I hope you don’t mind showing that interesting place to me,” said Sum Goh. “I should also like to see the garden.”

They passed out of the room together, leaving their venerable parents to entertain themselves as best they might. Lai Pek and Tua Sai immediately plunged into a discussion about the state of world markets and business in general, while their respective female counterparts held an animated conversation on topics addressing the high art of gastronomy.

The pond was as round an affair as possible; a long stone structure about a foot high was firmly planted near one edge and afforded a convenient seat for the two young people. The clear water, its softly rippling surface brightened by the gleaming rays of the sun, was deep enough at the centre to completely cover a man from head to toe, even if he were extraordinarily tall. Its bottom was clearly visible, with its brown sand and tiny boulders and some fish gliding along with most complacent placidity. Its bank was paved with fresh green herbage; a mango tree reflected its resplendent wealth of boughs, foliage, and fine fruit in the serene depth of the water.

“This is the pond that gave me my inspiration,” laughed Gek Kim. “Unfortunately there are no ducklings floating on it now, so the scene is incomplete.”

“The scene is perfectly charming as it is,” replied Sum Goh, “even without the ducklings; and your picture does full justice to its beauty—there is no doubt about that.”

“You are very complimentary indeed,” said Gek Kim.

“Tell me, if you don’t mind,” asked Sum Goh, “have you lived here all your life?”

"Not exactly. I was born here, to be sure; but during the last five years I have spent my time mostly in Kuala Lumpur in my uncle's house, and I seldom came back. I only returned about three weeks ago."

"Are you going away soon?"

"No. This time I intend to stay here a few months at least."

"I am very glad to hear this. You will permit our friendship, won't you?"

"Of course. I have no patience with the absurd separation of the sexes into two different worlds. Why should women be banished from men's society, as if their presence were a danger? I can't understand how such a notion ever obtained currency. It is so odd that I always laugh at it."

Sum Goh's eyes shone with eloquent admiration.

"You are a marvel!" he exclaimed enthusiastically. "The more I know you, the more you fill me with wonder at the breadth of your mind. It's a pity I did not have the fortune to meet you before."

He was rapidly rushing towards a whirlpool of adoration and unconsciously verifying the ancient dictum against which Gek Kim had just professed anger, that woman's presence was a danger.

"What they call the emancipation of women is all to the good," she said, her cheeks flushing with excitement as she proceeded, and poor Sum Goh was completely captivated by her heightened beauty. "I don't know how it is possible to live in an atmosphere of perpetual constraint. It is doubtful whether women of former ages ever felt any happiness at all. I can hardly believe it, though my mother says with emphatic conviction that she and her girlfriends were supremely happy in their domestic seclusion and peaceful household duties. If my mother were not such a truthful, honest person, incapable of lying, as I know her to be, I should be tempted to laugh rudely in her face. Poor Mother! But she is quite unshakeable in her conviction of the rightness of her belief."

"It must be because distance gilds the actual facts and makes them seem glamorous."

"That is it! If she could have experienced both kinds of life as a girl, I am sure she would not hesitate to denounce the one she did actually experience and which she thinks was so sunny and refined. Of course, that life did not expose women to any jarring unpleasantness from the outside world. I know very well that the world is not a bed of roses, and going out into the world does not mean going into paradise. Sometimes we experience chill winds of bitterness that would not blow through our cosy houses; but those are extremely bracing. I can conceive of nothing more hideous than the deadly monotony of peace and comfort. If I were forced to endure such an existence, I think even a major disaster would receive a hearty welcome from me as a pleasant change." She laughed with merriment as she tossed a stone into the pond, producing a transient splash. "That pond must feel gratitude towards me for arousing it from its sleepiness."

"I wouldn't go so far as to desire a calamity under any circumstances," said Sum Goh with a serious mien. "And I can't imagine any trouble falling to your lot; at any rate, I fervently hope you won't meet with any."

"You are extremely kind and funny also, if you will excuse my saying so. I can't say that I have ever encountered anything more serious than mere trifling vexations. But I assure you that I could endure any hardship, if it were to come my way. Now, let us take a look around the garden, as you wished."

They arose from their seat and took a leisurely tour among the trees and plants. A fresh breeze, loaded with the fragrance of the splendid blossoms that shone with a brilliant variety of forms and colour, gently swept the scene, providing a delicious coolness that mollified the increasing warmth of the sun. Sum Goh was woefully ignorant of even the names of the flowers, never having been interested in nature study; but he listened with unrivalled attention to Gek Kim's explanations concerning the essential characteristics of each type of flower. But his devoted appearance of profound interest lay not so much in a laudable desire for the acquisition of a new branch of knowledge as in the music of her speech, which seemed to his fervent mind to exceed even the music of the violin. His sole artistic interest lay in that instrument, from which he could manage to elicit a few popular tunes; he was inordinately proud of his powers as a violinist in an amateur musical band.

"The New Year will be here in five days' time. How do you propose to spend it, Miss Low?"

"Why, I have not thought of it at all. Well, I don't think I shall do anything or go anywhere in particular. The New Year is the same as any other day to me."

"Would you consider going out for a short ride with me on New Year's Day?"

"I don't mind, as I have nothing special to do. Now, I think we had better rejoin our people. They may think something has happened to us if we leave them too long."

On his way home, Sum Goh was lost in a brown study, apparently disinclined to reveal his thoughts.

"Well," said Lai Pek, after first clearing his throat with a short cough, "we have had an interesting visit."

"I like her," said Sum Goh, mumbling to himself.

"Like her?" exclaimed Lai Pek. "Who?"

"Miss Low," replied Sum Goh mechanically. Then he realised with a start that he had been inadvertently revealing his innermost thoughts. He looked uncomfortable while his parents glanced at each other. Since he had let the cat out of the bag, however, he did not mind continuing: "But I don't know whether she likes me or not. She has accepted my invitation to go out with me on New Year's Day, though."

"Really!" exclaimed his venerable father. "You seem to be getting on pretty fast, aren't you?" He leaned back against the cushion and laughed so long and so loud that it was evident he had never been amused to such an extent before.

The chauffeur turned round in surprise and narrowly missed colliding with a bullock cart that lumbered past them.

"Look where you are going!" shouted Lai Pek to the driver with utmost alarm, recovering from his vigorous fit of mirth. "Ai-ya! We might all have been killed."

"If we had been," said Mrs. Lee, "it would have been your fault for laughing so much. Sum Goh, she must like you or else she wouldn't go out with you."

Sum Goh blushed and maintained an uncomfortable silence, not only during the journey home, but throughout that entire day.

Chapter 8

The New Year

It was the day before the New Year, the last day of the twelfth moon, the occasion of a great festival, when people's hearts sang and laughed, their purse-strings were loosened, and all was mirth and confusion. The poorest persons had diligently scrimped and saved some cash through dreary months, only to spend it all during this short season of joy. Debts, whether they had endured for a week or ten months, were now paid, cheerfully or reluctantly as the case might be, with practically no dunning on the part of the creditors. Families, separated by distance and confined to their particular localities owing to the exigencies of their daily tasks, were temporarily reunited. Friends forgot their petty animosities and vexatious grievances, which had nearly culminated on more than one occasion in downright enmity, and joined their hands in fraternal concord. Though joy reigned supreme, a certain inhibitory force, indescribable yet easily felt, appeared in the atmosphere, an enveloping solemnity that was not at all apparent during the rest of the year. Even children were aware of its subtle influence, in spite of the fact that they enjoyed themselves thoroughly. They experienced some discomfort from the unwonted constraint they had to exercise over their spirits in obedience to the oft-repeated injunctions of their parents never to indulge in any mischief or quarrels during these few days, or else they would not receive any pocket money, which was always very important but especially so at this time of year, in light of the numerous things, especially crackers, to be bought.

Everyone was up early; the streets were thronged with people laden with sundry purchases, from candles and incense-sticks to legs of pork and screaming fowl. The market, filled with a deafening din and a strange mixture of smells, was rendered almost impassable by the mass of struggling humanity that had commenced to stream into its precincts from the early hour of four o'clock in the morning. The shops were equally busy. The provision stores were hung with rows and rows of dried ducks and sausages, stretching right over the heads of the pedestrians on the five-foot way. The fruit shops were stocked with oranges and pomeloes from South China and sugarcane dug straight from the earth, roots and leaves still intact. Watermelons with green skins and red hearts abounded, evidently in great demand.

Red was the predominant colour. New sheets of red paper, inscribed with words bearing beneficent meanings, were pasted on walls and over doorways and above the altar of every god; they were supposedly efficacious in bringing prosperity to the household and driving away evil of every kind to a safe distance. Red bunting waved over the lintels; parcels were wrapped in paper encircled with strips of red; money presents to children were enclosed in red packets. This warm, deep-red symbol of triumphant joy glowed in villages and towns, and faces flushed in harmony with the surroundings.

The house of Low Tua Sai was gaily bedecked with buntings and lanterns made of cloth painted with lengthy dragons spouting water from the clouds and gorgeous lotus flowers in full bloom. Directly facing the door in the front parlour was an altar, on which reposed a gilt wooden image of the household god. Tall candles burned steadily on either side, and glowing incense sticks filled the room with a heavy, fragrant odour. A low square table sat before the altar, adorned with a brocade curtain. Various dishes of delicate food, arranged in regular rows, completely covered its surface; tea and wine in tiny porcelain cups lined the edges. On the floor in an iron vessel lay a mass of gold paper, consisting of sheets rolled into hollow cylinders so that they might catch fire easily and be completely reduced to ashes.

Mr. and Mrs. Low, together with Gek Kim and their three other children, as well as some half a dozen relatives from other parts of the country, were gathered in the room. All of them bowed thrice before the god with due reverence, holding incense sticks in their hands and murmuring prayers for prosperity during the coming year. After a considerable interval, the gold paper was set alight. Tua Sai lit the crackers, throwing them into the air. They roared and spluttered, giving immense delight to the children. When the ceremony was over, the tables were cleared, and the family adjourned to the dining room and sat down to a glorious feast.

"Oh!" said Tua Sai, picking up a piece of roast pork as brown and tender as the most scrupulous epicure could possibly desire, "how fast the years fly! It seems but yesterday, although it is more than forty years now, that we three were children tumbling on the sand mounds and performing all sorts of fantastic, wild antics."

The three persons referred to included his two brothers, one of whom was inordinately tall and the other inordinately fat. Their features were remarkably alike, although their figures were so different.

"Those were indeed happy times," said the fat brother, who did not look as if he had ever met with troubled days, and his childhood happiness could certainly not surpass his present happiness—he ate and drank with an appetite that was, to say the least, remarkable.

"Although our father was poor, and we hardly ever had any luxuries, still we seemed to live in perpetual joy. The birds we shot with our precious catapults; the fish we caught in streams; the strange games we played, of which I cannot recollect a thing—what a pity that we must all grow old!"

"And the fights we fought," chimed in the tall brother, who, although he smoked opium and usually possessed a poor appetite, ate a credible amount on this occasion. Then, suddenly remembering that it was not desirable to have the children know that they also had been fighters in their time, he added, "But our fights were all sham fights. We never quarrelled at all."

The children listened in astonishment to the foregoing conversation—they found it hard to believe that their father and uncles were once upon a time as small as they were.

"What games did you play, Uncle?" asked the youngest child of the fat brother; he was their favourite uncle, as he was very liberal in his presents and always answered their questions with good humour. "Did you play leapfrog?"

"I certainly did," answered the fat brother. "Why, I loved it."

The children roared with merriment, and the youngest child was about to ask another question when the noodles arrived on the table, and he did not voice the words as he was anxious to put his tongue to better use. Fine noodles they were, with such a delicious smell, fried with shrimp, pork, eggs, crabs, and a host of other ingredients.

"Haven't you begun looking round for a bridegroom for Gek Kim yet?" asked the tall brother of Tua Sai.

Gek Kim blushed and laughed. "Don't talk nonsense, Uncle."

"It's not nonsense," said the tall brother with a serious mien. "It's the duty of every parent to get his daughter married as soon as possible."

"To get rid of her, I suppose, so that she might cease to be an encumbrance on him," said Gek Kim.

"You really have curious notions!" laughed Tua Sai with his mouth full. "Imagine my wishing to get rid of you!" He roared till he choked and was only saved from imminent death by a timely thump on the back, delivered with force by the fat brother.

"I dare say some parents desire to see their daughters married for that motive, especially if they are loaded with too many of them," said the tall brother, who did not perceive what there was to laugh about. "Daughters are by no means profitable, and if a man is poor, he can't afford to keep them forever."

"You seem to look upon children from a financial standpoint," said Gek Kim, looking a little piqued.

"And why not?" said the tall brother. "After all, economic considerations must govern men's conduct, whether they want to submit to them or not. I don't mean to say, however, that you should get married because your father must think of his finances. No. The chief reason why you, and every girl, should get married, if possible, is because—because it has always been the custom to do so," he concluded in an authoritative tone.

"I am glad that you don't give a worse reason than that, Uncle."

"Ahem!" said the fat brother. "Talking about marriage reminds me of the fact that sixteen men applied for my daughter, Joh Hua, before I found a suitable husband for her and, curse my judgment, he turned out as bad a son-in-law as I ever wish to see. A drunken good-for-nothing and—worst of all—an ungrateful fellow. His father has long ceased to have any dealings with him. For the sake of my daughter, I helped him innumerable times, and last month I heard people say that he called me a miserly old wretch. But I have always been an unlucky chap," he concluded with placid resignation.

"Wouldn't it be better if a girl were to make her own choice of the man she wants to marry?" asked Gek Kim with an air of unconcerned coolness.

"What!" exclaimed the tall brother, "a girl to choose her own husband! Monstrous! It is bad enough when a man wants to choose his own wife, but a girl! What about delicacy and modesty? I am afraid that the present generation is gone to the devil." He closed his eyes in agony.

"I don't mind Gek Kim's suggestion at all. I am quite disillusioned about the judgment of a parent," stated the fat brother ruefully.

"I confess that I have never thought about the marriage of Gek Kim. I have indulged her in so many things that I suppose that I shall never be able to intervene effectively between her and her choice, if she were to have one," said Tua Sai, smiling upon her daughter.

"You are always very good, Father," said Gek Kim happily.

The tall brother groaned but ceased to pursue the subject any further. As the meal came to an end, he quickly retired to lie on his bed with all the apparatus for the smoking of opium. The others went to rest, and some of them slept in order to wear off the effects of repletion.

The evening dragged on slowly, and midnight arrived. The moonless sky was very dark, and only a few stars were visible. The silence of the cool, dry night, was, however, shattered by the incessant roar of crackers bursting in all corners of the town. The inhabitants were ushering in the New Year.

Tua Sai and family again worshipped the household god, this time only with fruit, which was to be left on the table for four days before it could be removed. Beggars appeared in groups and called down blessings on the house and did not appear as miserable as usual. They were glad and merry; none of them departed without alms. A band of pipers, dressed in long green gowns and wide-brimmed hats, played a lively tune for a few minutes before strolling on to another scene of gaiety. Unlike the Pied Piper of Hamelin, they actually did collect a handsome sum from the townsfolk for their night's work and therefore were not disposed to pipe away all the children in the town, though a few urchins followed them from place to place, attracted by the music. But all ceremonies must come to an end, and after two hours of noise and smoke, the town was sound asleep.

Chapter 9

The Ride

The morning light, pale but rich in promise of an ampler bloom, trickled through the window and mantled the room. Gek Kim awoke and lay still for a moment, trying to recollect her faculties; she looked at the clock on the table—seven o'clock—and remembered that it was New Year's Day. She raised herself on her elbow and looked out; the sky bubbled with a mass of wavering clouds, white, golden and rosy, which in places had commenced to dissolve and disappear from sight. The lusty birds sang their notes of gladness, as if they too were aware that there was something significant going on that day. The flowers, burnished with soft, lucid dew, fluttered amid their retinue of green leaves in unison with the cool, fresh breeze. She arose and went downstairs where she found most of her family already up and about. They all wished her prosperity and happiness, and if words had any effect, her future was assured.

They all sported new clothes; even her father had donned a new pair of blue silk trousers, loose and airy. The children felt glorious in their array and were incessantly lighting crackers, vying with one another as to whose exploded with the loudest violence. They felt very opulent, as they were all stuffed with red packets from their parents and uncles. They were preparing to pay a round of visits to their parents' intimate friends and receive more red packets in return for ceremonious salutations.

After breakfast, a continual stream of visitors, male and female, arrived to exchange pleasant greetings; they each sat for a few minutes, enjoyed a cup of coffee and some cakes made by Mrs. Low herself, pronounced them delicious, and departed, leaving a most agreeable impression. Most of them withdrew hurriedly, as they were anxious to bring their round of visits to a speedy close so that they might devote the afternoon to games of chance. Indeed, in the eyes of many worthy persons, more than anything else this season of gaiety meant a period of intense gambling, relieved by feasting and drinking.

A visitor suggested a game of cards to Tua Sai.

"We can easily form a party of four—you, one of your brothers, and we two here," he remarked, indicating another visitor with a bloated face and a bald head.

"I have made it a rule never to gamble," declared the fat brother, "since a son of a friend of mine got into serious trouble three years ago. That friend was my neighbour, and we were on intimate terms. I knew how much he got from his father in order to indulge his madness. His father did what he could to cure him of this, from imploring him to think of the honourable name of his family to threatening to disinherit him. The son promised to reform innumerable times, but he never kept his word for long. At last his father told him he would not give him anything till he had really stopped his evil habit. Shortly afterwards, we were horrified to find that he was accused of breaking into a house at night and stealing a goodly sum of money. We could not believe it. But he fell under general suspicion because the evidence against him was too strong, and it was thought conclusive because he disappeared that very night. Even now I don't believe he was guilty. He could not have descended to such depths."

"What actually happened?" asked the visitor sympathetically.

"The occupant of the house he was alleged to have entered declared that he came upon the thief unawares as he was ransacking a safe. Before he could do anything, the neighbour was knocked senseless and the thief departed, before he could recognise his features."

"Hasn't he come back to his family since?"

"No; so far as I know, not once. They can't say whether he is dead or alive."

"That is a most unfortunate ending. His people must have received a terrible shock. But we play only once in a while, just for amusement, so I suppose there is no harm in it," smiled the visitor.

When all the guests had gone, the tall brother turned towards the fat brother with an annoyed countenance and demanded, "Why did you tell that story? Do you want to make our family lose face? Don't forget the excellent proverb, 'difficult it is for a team of four horses to chase a word which has left the mouth!' You are a chatterbox."

"I couldn't help it," groaned the fat brother. "Whenever I think of gambling I think of that horror. But I did not say that it was the son of our sister who was accused of being a robber."

"I had hoped that by this time the sordid story would have been forgotten by everybody who knew it."

"I have tried not to think of it. And yet—he was not a bad son. I think you must still remember him well, Gek Kim. You were sixteen then, and you had lived with us for two years already."

"Oh yes, I still remember him," replied Gek Kim. "I sometimes wonder what has happened to him. Why has he not communicated with us at all?"

"He must have been heartily sick of his career, and he is ashamed of presenting himself to us again."

"I wish you wouldn't talk about him any more," said the tall brother in a freezing tone.

Gek Kim vividly recalled this cousin of hers. He was rugged and muscular, with eyes that more often than not contained a hint of suppressed indignation, as if he were haunted by some perpetual grievance against the world.

They had seldom talked with each other because, though he lived in a neighbouring house, and she often went over to see her aunt, he was seldom at home. Her aunt, his mother, had died of grief shortly after the catastrophe, and his father had hardly ever smiled since that time. Her cousin was not, however, as her fat uncle had said, really wicked; on the few occasions he spoke to her he behaved very kindly, and except for that one ineradicable vice, he never did anything evil. But she soon ceased to think of the matter; her attention was distracted by a discussion between her uncles as to the merits of ducks' eggs versus hens' eggs.

"Ducks' eggs are bigger, and two of them contain as much substance as three hens' eggs," said the fat brother.

"Hens' eggs are tastier, smell better, and are far more wholesome," asserted the tall brother seriously. "Ducks' eggs can be preserved, and how nice preserved eggs taste! Preserved hens' eggs are practically unknown."

"I hate preserved eggs! You can eat hens' eggs half-boiled, and I can think of no better food."

Gek Kim laughed and left them to their debate.

In the afternoon, as she sat in a vague reverie, a hundred thoughts floating like gossamer in her mind, Sum Goh arrived in a car. He had called to take her out for a drive together.

"If I may be permitted to say so, Miss Low," remarked Sum Goh with sudden boldness as they were riding along a smooth, level highway shaded by tall angsana trees from which streams of soft yellow blossoms floated down with festal blitheness, "you look wonderful in your crimson dress."

She blushed but did not look at all displeased. She did not reply to his comment, however, but asked, "Where are we going now?"

"We shall take a leisurely survey of the town and then spin about the countryside. I presume you are not familiar with the village around here, are you?"

"No. I have seen only a few like Lopi, where I remember I saw nothing but groundnuts. The whole population was engaged in nothing but planting them in the fields or selling them in the shops. There were mounds of them."

They passed through the streets, entangled in a procession of cars and rickshaws containing masses of laughing people, riding about without any particular destination but only, as they expressed it, "to eat wind." In fact, they literally seemed to do so, as most of them kept their mouths open half the time. A certain last-year-has-gone-and-surely-fate-must-be-kinder-this-year philosophy sang in their hearts; and it might be true that, in the lives of many, unalloyed happiness was possible only during this brief period, when all the dictates of prudence and the consuming cares of daily occurrence were thrown to the winds and resolutely prohibited from entering the mind.

All the shops were closed, even the restaurants. It was curious to behold such throngs of humanity filling the streets while most houses had locked doors, so that the people appeared as if they had sprouted from the earth and not issued like ordinary work-a-day mortals from human habitations. The telephone wires overhead were lined with innumerable sparrows that, before they went to sleep, were chirping loquaciously and enjoying the spectacle below.

"Let's drive around the lakes," suggested Sum Goh, as they emerged from the crowd of vehicles. "It's suffocating to breathe the dust in this warm atmosphere and to crawl along so slowly."

The scenery was superb. The clear water rippled serenely with rhythmic sounds, and the verdant banks teemed with glorious flowers. They enjoyed a tour of the countryside, passing through several villages whose inhabitants were, if anything, happier than the townsfolk. Some of these villages were noted for particular products—one possessed a special reputation for its coir mats, another for rambutans, and a third for the production of bean curds, which were so good that no one ever passed through the place without carrying a certain quantity away.

After rattling over an iron bridge that traversed a river filled with sampans, they arrived at a place that was a cross between a village and a town. Sum Goh slowed down a bit.

"A remarkable old man lives in this spot, which is known as Toliu," he said. "I know him quite well. He used to live in Lanta and possessed a great reputation for his skill in medicine and horoscopy. Everybody who wanted to cure some bodily ailment or to feel reassured about his future fortune consulted him. The success of his bodily cures was only rivalled by that of his prognostications. Our family relied absolutely upon his prescriptions. I grew up on his medicines and his predictions. As far back as I can remember he was already an old man. He must have collected a modest fortune from his work, but he always lived simply. He retired here half a dozen years ago and now lives in a solitary house, little more than a hut, by himself. He has always been partial to me, for some unknown reason, but I have seen him rarely since he left us. I still remember him with affection. You might be interested to see him. At any rate, I should pay my respects to him now that I am here."

They soon came in sight of a small house, which stood isolated a few paces from its neighbours. A venerable, patriarchal figure sat on the five-foot way, smoking a water pipe; his white beard, smoothed to a fine point, rested upon his bosom in placid repose. He wore a black wooden ring on the second finger of his right hand, and he was without an upper garment. In spite of his years, he looked robust, and his face exhibited a humorous lightness that was quite inconsistent with the gravity of his former calling.

"Aged Uncle!" shouted Sum Goh while he was still on the road. "Abundant happiness and scores of years be yours!"

"Oh! Is that you, Sum Goh?" asked the patriarch, sincere pleasure lighting up his eyes. "Why, I have not seen your pleasant self for more than a year, since you came here with your father to consult me when your little brother was rather seriously ill. How are your father and mother getting on, and your brothers and sisters?"

"They are all in good health, Aged Uncle. May I introduce this young lady? Her family and ours are on friendly terms."

"Welcome, esteemed lady. What is your father's great name?

"Low Tua Sai, Aged Uncle."

"Oh! I remember, but somehow or other we came in little contact. Come in and rest a while before you proceed on your journey."

The room was almost devoid of furniture and by no means very clean. When they were all seated, the old man said, addressing himself to Gek Kim, "Oh! How pleasant it is to be young, with all life opening up before you. From your face I can see that you are destined to a long career of happiness. Let me read your horoscope, if you don't mind." He became full of professional interest. "For years, I have desisted from my previous employment. I have not read anyone's fortune for a long time now; but I will look into yours, as I think your future is going to be unusually interesting"

"Really, Aged Uncle, you make me feel important," said Gek Kim.

"You are really a remarkable soothsayer, Uncle," chimed in Sum Goh. "It's a pity you ceased to practise. There is no one else like you."

"Ai-ya! You are too complimentary!" exclaimed the patriarch, extremely pleased. "If I were to tell people what you tell me, they would undoubtedly retort, 'If this red turnip of yours is lacking, will one be unable to prepare food?' Just supply me with the date and hour of your birth," he concluded, turning towards Gek Kim.

He retired into an inner chamber to consult his learned treatises, and after a certain interval of time had elapsed, he emerged with a slip of paper in his hand, on which he had scribbled some characters. "I find that before you attain your heart's desire, you will fall into the grasp of a crocodile. He will endeavour to devour you, but you will not wholly pass into his capacious belly. He is destined to release you when you are only half within his jaws."

"How frightful!" murmured Gek Kim with a shudder, real or feigned—it was difficult for Sum Goh to determine. "What does it mean, and when is this terrible misfortune due to happen?"

"It will occur during the course of this year. Literally it means that you will suffer an unpleasant calamity. But don't worry. You will be safe in the end, and your desire will be fulfilled."

"That is a great comfort, at any rate, Aged Uncle. We must be moving on. Thank you for your hospitality and your skilled prophecy."

The dusk was gathering fast as they left the venerable prognosticator behind them, smoking his pipe with a contemplative mien.

"What do you think of the prediction?" asked Sum Goh.

"It's all nonsense, of course. With all due respect for his age and his evident affection for you, I must confess I don't believe a word of it."

"I wouldn't go so far as to say that he is absolutely wrong. Too many of his prophecies have been fulfilled."

"And how many have been unfulfilled? We are struck only by those that come to pass and conveniently forget the rest. Besides, what he says is extremely vague. An impending calamity. Misfortunes happen so often that there is nothing remarkable if some should turn out according to prophecy. I have an aunt who is tremendously fond of having her fortune told. The moment she hears that there is somebody somewhere or other who has a reputation for some kind of divination, she will hurry to him. She has consulted I don't know how many geomancers, augurs, astrologers, necromancers, palmists, and wizards, and the curious thing is that almost all of them promised her whatever she hoped for. She was either going to attain her wish in the near future or else she was fated to suffer for a while before prosperity came back. At any rate, adversity never lasted long. And so far, some of her many desires have come to pass as predicted, but her chief yearning has remained ungratified."

"And what was her chief yearning?"

“To give birth to a boy, but fate has obstinately refused to grant her anything but girls. She has seven of them.”

“I am afraid you are a hopeless sceptic. But for once I hope the soothsayer is wrong. I don’t cherish the idea of your being bitten by even an ant, much less devoured by a crocodile, even though for some strange reason it has to belch you up again.”

“Thank you for your considerateness,” she said sweetly. “I forgot to ask the venerable old man what my dearest wish was. I have myself no idea of its existence. He said that before I attained my heart’s desire I was to meet the crocodile—to make the desired object much more tempting, I suppose. I have never had any consuming wish of any sort. I wonder what this one can be that is so hard to obtain?”

“I have no doubt upon the subject of my greatest desire,” said Sum Goh wistfully.

He turned his head to have a good look at her. She instantly averted her face and became absorbed in contemplation of the dark road they were traversing. The prospect seemed to be very enchanting, as she remained silent. The town was brilliantly lit when they reached home, and it received two people who each secretly thought that they had spent a very pleasant day indeed.

Chapter 10

Competition

As the days passed, Beng Hu's commercial prosperity increased immensely. It did not progress in gradual, imperceptible stages but arose all of a sudden, like the stately palace erected for Aladdin by his memorable genie. His firm became the emporium of the town—the envy and admiration of all mortals, the sensation of the year—and its fame quickly spread in all directions. Besides selling by retail, it also provided the stock for the small shops, both in the town and the villages. Credit was freely given, and the instalment system made it tempting for every householder to become a patron. When a person wished to go out shopping and was asked, "Where are you going?" he would in all probability reply, "The Fleet Horse, of course."

Beng Hu's personal popularity was in direct proportion to his business success. Like an algebraic relationship between two quantities, the two varied directly with each other; but in his case, the quantities showed a phenomenal increase between successive stages. When the lightning flashes, thunder follows. The club was sadly incomplete without his gracious presence, and he was invited to all the weddings and parties within a radius of ten miles.

Poor people approached him for advice on all sorts of private troubles, and his decisions were acclaimed as models of wisdom and justice. An old man came to him with the complaint that his unfilial son, who was a motorcar driver, refused to support him in his decrepitude but preferred to squander his earnings on some loose woman, and Ben Hu conscientiously interviewed the unnatural son and persuaded him to return to a more graceful state of behaviour. A husband and wife had quarrelled, and the ungallant male was desirous of a divorce, declaring that he could secure a younger and handsomer wife in no time, but they were soon reconciled and lived in harmony. A mining coolie lamented that he had deposited two years' savings with a certain respectable shopkeeper. The shopkeeper now declined to return the requisite sum, averring that he had never received anything and demanded that the coolie produce his bond as evidence. In such a case it was impossible to force the unscrupulous shopkeeper to acknowledge his guilt, as he would have lost face had he taken such an unwise step. The sympathetic Beng Hu therefore recompensed the coolie for his undeserved loss, and the poor fellow was so overcome by gratitude that he would have prostrated himself on the ground before his benefactor, had the custom not become obsolete.

It was undoubtedly only a matter of a year or two, as his well-wishers stoutly maintained, before he would be unanimously elected head of the community, and he might even aspire to the exalted glory of a justice of the peace. He made munificent donations to various charitable enterprises, from private schools to funds for the relief of the flood victims in China. There was a movement afoot to add a pagoda to the local temple, and he was honoured for making the most substantial contribution to the project by having his portrait placed in a conspicuous position on the third tier for every visitor to behold. He received honour and vast profit with the right hand and gave away a generous portion of the latter with the left, to the considerable augmentation of the former.

He was also noted for his hunting. Beng Hu dauntlessly ventured into an unhealthy swamp to exterminate a man-eating crocodile that had recently devoured an unfortunate boy. He specialized in wild boars. Once a fortnight he would penetrate the recesses of the forest and bring home with him the carcass of one of those unprepossessing creatures, whose meat, however, he did not relish but bestowed, free, on those who loved its taste. He hunted them, as he said, because of the thrill and the fact that he thoroughly detested the tusked monsters since the day that one of them gored his leg, inflicting a wound whose unsightly scar was still in evidence.

Three months later, once his provision store was a roaring success, he hit upon a brilliant idea that made him still more popular. Passing through a yam plantation one day while returning home from a hunting expedition, he paused to mop his brow and survey the scene. A shining thought floated into his mind—this must have been due to the influence of his beneficent ancestors, ever solicitous of his welfare. The more he contemplated the idea, the more pleasing it became. He lost no time in giving his project substantial form. He secured the services of the best confectioner he could find and, together with him, created a requisite product. Yam was beaten into a paste, and rice flour and other ingredients were mixed in subtle proportions to form a crisp, dry tickler of the palate. These were packed in tins and sold at a popular price; they were even exported to distant towns. They were the delight of both rich and poor and were eaten at breakfast, lunch, and dinner. Picnics were decidedly less enjoyable without their soothing taste. They were the last thing taken at night, a better soporific than potassium bromide. They were the glory of the table.

But, as is the lamentable fact in many branches of human activity and especially in commerce, the gain of one person often involves loss for another, and many traders in the town found their businesses adversely affected. Lai Pek, holding a distinguished position, found himself hardest hit of all. His sales and profits showed an unwelcome decline, and he was at first annoyed and then later alarmed by this unprecedented, unattractive result. He became more splendidly energetic than ever. He endeavoured to stimulate interest in his goods with a grand sale lasting a month, but this did not secure him any ultimate advantage; the moment the sale was over, his business returned to its previous deplorable condition. He began to nurse a hearty dislike of the unfavourable effect on his established concern in so short a space of time. His smug self-satisfaction was shaken: water evaporates near a fire.

As he sat in unbecoming dejection, pondering over his grievances and racking his brain to discover a path that might perchance lead him out of the jungle of his difficulties, he was confronted by the smiling Hwey Pin, whose loud, "Have you eaten rice, Lai Pek?" startled him.

"Yes," feebly smiled Lai Pek. "And you?"

"I ate three bowls just now," replied the other with untimely jocularity. "What's the matter with you? You look as if you had produced a string of daughters."

"I haven't been feeling well these last few days." He suppressed a rising sigh. "The rainy weather is most disagreeable."

"I never knew you to be affected by rain before."

"My constitution has weakened considerably."

"Better eat ginseng. I have a few words to say to you. You are not too ill to listen, are you?

"No, carry on."

"You have noticed, I dare say, the astounding success of Sin Beng Hu. You may or may not have discovered that many worthy shopkeepers have been injured by his prosperity."

"To take you into my confidence, I myself am among that unfortunate number."

“The head of a hare and the eyes of a snake make up his appearance,” said Hwey Pin with venom. “As if he has not done enough harm already, he has established a confectionery for the production of yam cakes. This new enterprise does not indeed affect our business to such an extent as his other goods. But all the same, it’s annoying.”

“I am of the same opinion.”

“Why should we not put our heads together and devise a way to defeat him?”

“My incapable brain has in vain searched for an adequate method.”

“I have thought it over for some time, and I think this scheme is the best. We should also open a confectionery.”

“This won’t do; it’s pure imitation. People will laugh at us, and besides, being first in the field, his stuff has acquired too great a reputation to be shaken.”

“We need not make yam cake. I am thinking of potato cake.”

“What!” Lai Pek started. “What kind of potato cake?”

“An absolutely new variety. Many people prefer potatoes to yams.”

“I am afraid this scheme is impractical. I haven’t sufficient capital to enable me to launch into this new business.”

“I have thought of a way to obtain sufficient funds. We can secure the cooperation of some of those whose business Sin Beng Hu has damaged. You can be the chief partner. If you don’t mind, I’ll be the manager.”

“If this venture does not succeed, it will make my position worse.”

“It can’t fail. Our cake is sure to be much more popular than his. I have the word of one of the best cake-makers in the country.”

“Well then, I hope we succeed. I don’t mind losing a bit if we can in any way humiliate him.”

And so, a short time later, the inhabitants of Lanta were agreeably astonished to find a new variety of cake offered for their consumption. The price was very low, sold at cost, in fact, according to the proprietors of the Avenging Lion. The fickle populace for a time abandoned yam cake in favour of potato cake because of its cheapness and newer flavour. Lai Pek and associates laughed joyously as they counted the proceeds and found their losses more than repaired; Hwey Pin congratulated himself on his idea and did not fail to point out to Lai Pek his conspicuous share in the inception of the project.

Beng Hu was profoundly incensed at this unforeseen opposition to his enterprise, as it appeared to him wholly unprovoked and a flagrant instance of dishonourable conduct. The name his rivals chose to bestow on their company was an insult and obviously indicated that their bosoms were filled by some unaccountable feeling of hostility towards him. He did not like to live in an unfriendly atmosphere, amid covert looks of malice. But he was resolved not to allow such ill-natured triumph to last forever. He made a drastic reduction in the price of his product and improved its quality.

The town rang with intense competition between the two companies and was provided with a staple topic of conversation, which never failed to evoke gigantic amusement. The population divided itself into two mildly contentious camps: yam-cake eaters and potato-cake eaters. The former regarded the latter with a noticeable sneer of refined irony, hinting that the others must be endowed with asinine faculties. The members of the latter category did not scruple to broadcast their belief that there undoubtedly existed, although most unfortunately, many otherwise normal human beings who were as deficient in the gustatory senses as the swinish tribe and were fit only to eat refuse, not rice. Persons of cultivated politeness exchanged covert repartees on the subject—they were themselves astonished at the brilliance they produced, and some awoke to the pleasant discovery that they were wits. Street hooligans and those not so versed in the ambiguous meanings of phrases and the subtleties of language, after a heated argument, sometimes proceeded to exchange resounding blows.

The popularity of both products was equally balanced, and neither of the two competitive companies could extinguish the flame of the other. Hwey Pin decidedly enjoyed the contest, but admittedly the two principal protagonists in the drama did not relish it to any appreciable extent—Beng Hu because the affair was rapidly sliding into the vulgar and bellicose, and he was haunted by the fear that warring gangs might be the result, not because he was devoid of physical courage but because he desired to live in peace if possible, and Lai Pek because the systematic reduction in prices might lead to a condition of bankruptcy if the contest were indefinitely prolonged. In any case, his real business did not receive much benefit; his store did not recover its former prosperity. But neither was willing to give way to the other, and a compromise was unthinkable; each considered that the other had done him such wrong that he was not disposed to be on harmonious terms with him. And so the strife was perforce maintained.

Chapter 11

The Procession

The cordial relationship between Sum Goh and Gek Kim was immensely strengthened as day succeeded day and visit followed visit; but there was yet no talk of a ceremonial betrothal, which would have been highly pleasing to their respective families. The bold word was not spoken, as Sum Goh still could not propose to her in a direct manner. He had to place feeble reliance on hints and the expressive language of the eyes, which—oh, misery of miseries!—were inexplicably lost on the girl, who either through innocence or pretence made no suitable response to entitle him to tread another step up the ladder of matrimonial conversation. Sometimes he began to harbour apprehensions that there was some special reason behind her friendship that did not possess the remotest connection with his objective. He wondered whether it would not have been simpler and less troubling and vexatious to follow what had happened to some of his friends—their parents had arranged their weddings for them by dispatching go-betweens to the parents of the prospective brides. His own parents had in fact suggested that, in accordance with the proprieties, they dispatch a go-between to her parents to make a formal request. Sum Goh had, however, declined to consider the idea of a go-between. He groaned at his predicament. As a result of his timorous indecision, unflattering comments and allusions were circulated concerning their constant presence in each other's company; people remarked that there was something suspicious when two young, unmarried people were forever being seen together. They looked forward with anticipatory smiles to some scandal.

Gek Kim was blissfully unaware of the sensation she was creating; even if it had been told to her, it was improbable that insomnia would have visited her. She was not at all romantic and hitherto thought little of love or marriage. She understood Sum Goh's intentions quite well and liked him very much. But she resolved to prolong their acquaintance a little and learn more of his character before she committed herself. "A most unlovely trait indeed," asserted one of her friends, who had been engaged to a man the day after she saw him, "absolutely unlike the romantic idea of impetuous love," when Gek Kim revealed the nature of her attitude towards Sum Goh in response to her friend's persistent questioning.

A great festival was held at periodic intervals of a good number of years in the city-port of Bitung in honour of Kuan Yin, the Goddess of Mercy. Its immense popularity was greatly enhanced by a procession, whose reputation for brilliance was the highest in the country. Devotees, who journeyed there for worship, and sightseers, who merely wanted to view the procession, flocked from all parts of the land and thronged the city. Sum Goh suggested that both their families should travel there together, and his proposal was enthusiastically accepted. Lai Pek, to kill two birds with one stone, also discovered that he had some business to transact with a cloth merchant in the city, and he was pleased to be able to enjoy the famous spectacle as well.

On the appointed day, Lai Pek and family, together with Tua Sai and family, gathered on the platform of the local railway station, waiting with some impatience for the train to arrive. The platform was positively choked with people—a vaster crowd than had been seen for years. It was fully five minutes before Sum Goh succeeded in booking the tickets from the haughty clerk, whose nerves had been badly frayed by the rush and whose temper verged more towards irritable than usual. Their train, which was scheduled to arrive three minutes after another going in the opposite direction, was to stop at the second platform, which passengers were officially requested to reach by traversing an overhead bridge. The sky was overcast; large thunder-bearing clouds were gathering ominously, and it had just begun to drizzle slightly. Lai Pek, always more afraid of raindrops than of heavy showers, as the former were supposed to more easily produce colds, thought it would be more convenient to cross the railway lines.

"Hey, you!" shouted the station master, dressed in white drill uniform, with stentorian, official dignity, when Lai Pek's right foot was just raised in the act of stepping over the first line. "Come back! You are infringing on regulations."

"I'll just run over," said Lai Pek in undignified confusion. "It's raining."

"Use an umbrella. Come back immediately."

A bulky policeman took two steps forward; Lai Pek hastily stepped back and abandoned his ignominious attempt to commit a flagrant breach of law. Like the others without umbrellas, the cool, refreshing rain fell on his head during the two minutes it took to walk the bridge.

And the train was late. The passengers began to speculate on the causes of the delay; information was sought from porters, who shook their heads and offered no reply. Presently it transpired that the train had collided with a buffalo four miles away; the animal was killed and the engine damaged.

"Most unfortunate," murmured Tua Sai, but whether he was referring to the engine or the buffalo or their party for having to wait an indefinite interval, he did not explicitly say. What with the rain and the delay, his enthusiasm for the journey perceptibly waned. They formed a rather ominous prelude to the visit, and Tua Sai began to rack his brain for any other portents. He suddenly recollected a vivid dream he had had the previous night—a bee stung his finger and, flying away hastily, knocked its head against a tree and dissolved into a cloud. The bee bore reference to the train, the cloud to the rain, and the dream was fulfilled. He related his dream and his fears that the proposed visit was inauspicious, but Gek Kim, with unfilial lack of respect, exclaimed impatiently, "Don't be ridiculous!"

He walked away and became silent.

The train steamed in at last, after nearly everyone had lost patience and some were beginning to think of returning their tickets. Sum Goh was the last of the party to enter the carriage. The guard blew his whistle and waved his green flag with an air of importance, and the train roared. Its clumsy length stirred, and it continued its winding journey. The clouds loosened their store of rain, which added pleasing sounds to those of the train to produce a harmonious, soothing effect. Tua Sai began to nod before the train had run for half an hour, in spite of his preoccupation with his prophetic dream. Both Mrs. Lee and Mrs. Low had brought lunch baskets, and the children periodically enjoyed the contents; the adults either had no desire for food or did not feel inclined to make unlovely movements of the mouth before so many staring strangers.

At more or less regular intervals of three or four miles, they passed through a succession of stations, small stations with brick roofs and concrete pavements, bordered by ground strewn with red earth and planted with flowers like the hibiscus. They rolled through sleepy villages, whose inhabitants all temporarily paused from their work and turned their faces towards the passing carriages with smiling interest, making conversation among themselves, some of which might have related to the passengers and might not have been wholly flattering.

“How pleasant it is to live in a village,” remarked Mrs. Low turning from the window, through which she had been gazing for some time. “The people are all so friendly. They know one another thoroughly and spend their time in enjoyable conversation and a little work. They do not quarrel; they have no cares.”

“I don’t know what they have to talk about,” said Gek Kim unpleasantly. “And I am sorry that they are by no means as happy as you think. You have only to look at their faces to see that they have their own troubles to worry about.”

“A village is an excellent place for a married couple who love each other. They have no distractions to wean them from their mutual company,” put in Sum Goh wistfully.

He thought he detected a glimmer of amusement in Gek Kim’s scintillating eyes and felt crushed.

The heavy rain ceased. The sun burst out in all its brilliance, Tua Sai awoke, and the train reached the town of Kree, where it discharged all its passengers, who then had to embark in a launch and cross on a ferry in order to reach the city. The ferry was soon packed to full capacity and began to move with tolerable speed. The sampans and tongkangs rocked and heaved, and sailing vessels travelled on their sides, inclined at perilous angles, their sails distended to bursting point. But the ocean liners out at sea rode calm and majestic. While Lai Pek was gazing at them with intense interest, the launch reached the pier. The clock tower sounded two ringing notes as they reached the road. The officious rickshaw-pullers began to shout and snatch at their bags before their services were requested; when their prospective fares drove off in two taxis instead, they were left behind to curse and swear. The vehicles moved along very slowly, for the traffic was heavy. The unusually merry crowds roared and jostled, and a thriving business was carried on at the roadside stalls, many of which sold food and noodles and were hung with raw, red pork, boiled prawns, and vegetables; the frying pans sizzled and spluttered; the customers squatted on benches or sat at untidy little wooden tables. The party secured accommodation on the second storey of a hotel at double the customary rate.

The procession was scheduled to move along the streets for three alternate days, starting at noon each day and ending at midnight. The intended travel route was posted beforehand. It formed the principal topic everywhere: the next road it would appear in, the merits and demerits of its various attractions, and the comparison of the latter with those of former years, usually to the current year's manifest disadvantage. But this did not trouble the younger people, who possessed only a hazy recollection of the previous one, if they had seen it at all, which occurred more than ten years ago.

Sum Goh, who seemed to be dealing out all the suggestions relating to their plans, decided that they should venture out at eight o'clock in the evening and intercept the procession in Middle Street, as it would not pass by their temporary residence, which was situated on the outskirts of the town. It must be admitted that Gek Kim spent an undue amount of time over her toilette on this occasion, but when she issued from her room robed in a glossy pink satin dress, she became the pleasing focus of all eyes, an honour that Sum Goh by no means liked her to receive. His possessive instincts were aroused, yet, curiously enough, he also felt that it was absolutely wonderful to be seen together with a woman of such exquisite grace. Behind his assumed mask of impassivity, two conflicting emotions wrestled, with equal balance of power. "What a glorious girl!" he overheard one stranger remark to another in a tone intended to be a murmur, but which, perhaps because the speaker was slightly deaf, was quite audible, and he felt the height of happiness and the depth of misery at the same time. She had also caught the remark and, with a slight colouring round her ears, she turned towards Sum Goh with a faint smile. What did that smile mean? He pondered. Did she want him to knock the speaker down for his impertinence? He was quite ready to perform that feat, although when he looked at the stranger's large physique he quailed somewhat. Or was she pleased at the tribute to her beauty? Before he could solve the tormenting dilemma, they were in the midst of a roaring crowd, all hurrying in the direction of Middle Street.

When they reached their destination, they found an advantageous position on the first floor of a restaurant; their table was near a window, which was thrown wide open onto a commanding view of the scene below.

There was a quarter of an hour more before the procession would appear, but its drums were heard, emitting clamorous sounds from the next road. Both sides of the street were closely lined with swaying masses struggling to stand in front. Lai Pek ordered chrysanthemum tea as a prelude to the meal that would ensue. One single pot sufficed for the whole party; boiling water was continually added to the leaves until the decoction finally lost its fragrance. Before each person was a tiny bowl to hold the food and a tinier cup to hold the tea. The dishes that followed were substantially large and bore a greasy appearance. They were placed in the centre of the table in regular succession, and as a serving dish appeared, all dipped their chopsticks and spoons into the mass, each gathering a portion that was then placed in the small bowl. Lai Pek was the heartiest eater and systematically scraped out the remains of a dish before it was carried away. Dumplings, shark fins, birds' nests, and stewed duck, which were almost entirely consumed by Tua Sai, made their separate appearances. They ate and watched the procession at the same time, and whichever was the more appealing at a particular moment received the most consideration. Sum Goh and Gek Kim touched the dishes rarely but instead directed their attention to the spectacle below.

The procession was more than a mile and a half long and took nearly two hours to pass by. It travelled at a speed comparable to that of a tortoise, making frequent pauses either to take a breath or because something had gone wrong in some part of its unwieldy length. It was composed of contingents sent by various corporations and clubs that vied with one another as to the impressive beauty of the display they could create. Each section, headed by a banner inscribed with the distinguished name of the body it represented, was followed by a troupe of musicians and more banners, and terminated in a decorated vehicle that formed the chief attraction and on which the greatest amount of painstaking artistry and unstinted expenditure had been lavished. Between the company sections rolled unsavoury-looking carts, bearing refreshments to revive the energies of the faint and faltering.

"Here comes the procession!" exclaimed Mrs. Lee enthusiastically. "The first company is the rubber merchants' association. Look how tall that banner is!"

The pole was indeed so long and heavy that in order to keep it erect the carrier was running from side to side, as if he were executing some special dance.

"What a beautiful pageant!" exclaimed Mrs. Low, straining her eyes to their fullest extent.

An elaborate superstructure was erected above a motor lorry, carefully rigged out with artificial flowers, birds and two lions turning their gilt countenances to the crowd on either side, with large heads, thin bodies, and an awe-inspiring quantity of flowing mane—which would have looked more lifelike if they did not appear to have sustained a prolonged fast. At the very apex sat a girl of ten, who did not look at all merry, although she had never been so well apparelled in her life, set up to represent some legendary beauty who became the goddess of a star in the remote past.

"The spectacle is so much more glamorous at night," said Mrs. Lee. "The effect of those many tiny electric lights dotting the structure is marvellous. Look at those two attached to the ears of the girl."

Next followed the contributions from the butchers' association, the musical club, the peach-blossom club, the clan organisations, and a host of associations, great and small.

"How funny!" laughed Mrs. Low. "Look at the old uncle and the old aunt."

A supposedly old couple rode in rickshaws, holding an altercation characteristic of the general tenor of their life, and the lady was systematically knocking the head of her hen-pecked spouse with a good stout bamboo pole, whose resounding cracks seemed neither to restrain his loquacity nor make him commit any retaliatory action.

"This is the most splendid spectacle of all!" Tua Sai almost shouted, waving his arms in an outburst of generous enthusiasm. "It will undoubtedly win first prize. The goldsmiths' association! Oh, no wonder!"

In a picturesque group were three beautiful, enchanting damsels, of whom the principal was supposed to stand on the crest of a very high wave, with the other two similarly poised on either side, occupying lower waves. They shone with gold, diamonds, and jade, wore gorgeous head-dresses, and carried wands adorned with bunches of long, glittering hair, which they gracefully waved about their engaging persons.

Then came a company of jovial persons wearing umbrella-like multi-coloured suits and rainbow-tinted knitted belts; straw hats hung at their backs. One hand carried a banner and the other held a huge cheroot, a foot long. They walked with unnaturally long strides, pausing at intervals to exchange uncommonly fine extemporaneous jokes, judging from the uncontrollable fits of thunderous laughter that rocked the bystanders.

"I wonder what they are laughing about," said the exasperated Lai Pek. "I should like to go down and listen to the jokers."

"By the time you reach the road, that company will have gone," responded Mrs. Lee.

"I wish I could hear the jokes."

"I never knew you were so fond of jokes."

"Not as a rule, but I have come here especially to enjoy myself and I don't want to miss any fun."

"You are enjoying yourself very much, aren't you?"

This undignified squabble between his parents, though trifling, was highly annoying to Sum Goh, especially in the presence of his love. To cover his embarrassment he said, "How have you found the procession, Miss Low?"

"I have seldom enjoyed myself so much." Her sparkling eyes and glowing cheeks confirmed her words.

She looks more wonderful than usual, he thought. "Look at that long boat." He pointed an impressive finger.

Around a carriage was constructed a frame shaped like a boat, bearing decorations of gilt fabric bulbs arranged to form patterns, plants, and creatures, which were rather cloying and brought forth critical remarks on account of flaws and omissions rather than praise. Two rows of gaily dressed musicians sat on the sides, playing their instruments and leaving the oars untouched. "It's splendid, but because of those oars hanging rigidly without a single hand resting on any of them, it doesn't have the appearance of a boat rowing along. It would be much more attractive if they were done away with. Then we could imagine it to be a fairy craft sailing along the clouds."

“Is the procession coming to an end?” asked Gek Kim.

“Yes,” Sum Goh replied, leaning far out of the window. “This is the last pageant. Look! The spider queen in the middle of her silvery web. The girl looks tired, though. It must be a nuisance to wear all that heavy stuff—the headdress, the clothes and jewels—and to sit there hour after hour. I shouldn’t like to be in her place.”

“Nobody wants you to do so,” chimed in Lai Pek.

The procession ended with the benign image of Kuan Yin. As the carriage bearing the deity rolled along with majestic pomp, devout devotees, chiefly of the female gender, fervently prayed with incense sticks, which they afterwards placed in front of her. Crackers were occasionally discharged, and the last trace of the procession moved slowly out of sight. A goodly proportion of the crowd hurried away to other parts of the town for yet another view of the spectacle. Lai Pek and Tua Sai stretched their cramped limbs, vigorously stamping their feet to get rid of pins and needles.

“We seem to have been here for untold hours,” remarked Lai Pek, as they emerged into the street, still reeking with smoke and overrun with cars, rickshaws, bicycles, and gesticulating throngs.

When they were near the door of her room, about to part for the night, Gek Kim said sweetly to Sum Goh, “Thank you for your suggestion that we should come here. I have seen a memorable sight.”

Her face looked perfectly fascinating in the dark corridor, illuminated only by a faint light at the other end, and she was more than usually gentle. It would have been scandalous if they had lingered there for any length of time, and she was preparing to enter her room. But a sudden bold resolution seized hold of Sum Goh; her graciousness completely deprived him of his shyness, and he opened his mouth to declare his passion, no doubt with eloquent and beautiful phrases, romantic to the last degree. While his mouth was open, before any fine words had time to issue forth, like a stream of liquid gold sliding smoothly down a shining hill of jade, a most untoward, though very commonplace and trifling, incident occurred. A waiter passed by him with a flask in one hand. Sum Goh closed his mouth and waited for him to disappear.

"See you tomorrow," said Gek Kim in her entrancing voice as she quickly entered her room. Sum Goh heard her lock the door.

As he walked towards his room, he felt mortified and began to analyse his attitude rigorously. *I behaved like a tremendous fool,* he told himself bitterly. Surreptitiously, the thought crept into his mind that the ancient method of purchasing brides might be much better—it probably entailed less worry for the man. Instead of hanging around a girl in a helpless manner, the best way of winning a wife might be to seize her by force, either through the power of a strong physique, as among savages, or through the hardly less effective power of gold, a method in vogue since civilisation began. The latter perfectly combined the advantages of force with apparent willingness on the part of the victim. He felt ashamed of his momentary notions, however, in light of Gek Kim and her special character. When he contemplated the future he felt thoroughly miserable. As he climbed into his bed, he resolved to propose to her on the following day, come what might.

Chapter 12

The Monastery

"Where do you desire to go this morning, Mrs. Low?" inquired Mrs. Lee, as the party assembled to discuss their immediate plans.

"I should like to go and worship in the Temple of Kuan Yin."

"That's excellent. I'll accompany you. The place is sure to be very lively."

"Are you going to offer prayers to the goddess or to see people?" asked Lai Pek sarcastically.

"Are you suggesting that I have no interest in the Goddess of Mercy?"

"Oh no! How can that be? A woman must be extremely abnormal if she did not believe in her."

"Do you mean to imply that she inspires no faith in you? Don't tell me that you are trying to be blasphemous!" exclaimed his spouse with solemn indignation.

"I? Why, I have burned several packets of incense sticks to her, especially when I felt slightly ill and feared I might get worse."

"I shall cross on the ferry to go and see a friend," said Tua Sai.

"And the most profitable way in which I could spend my time would be to finish the business that brought me," stated the ever-practical Lai Pek.

"What about us?" Sum Goh asked Gek Kim.

"Let's go and see places."

"What places?" asked Lai Pek.

"The noted hills here, say. Then there is the famous monastery in Yapi."

"Both beautiful spots," said Sum Goh. "When do we start?"

"The earlier the better—before it gets too hot."

They were going to be alone in each other's company. He remembered last night's resolution; he must propose to her today. The feat seemed rather more difficult, however, in broad daylight than under benevolent night.

Their vehicle soon left the town and reached the open country.

"There are the hills," said Sum Goh. "It must be delicious to live there."

They climbed onto the hill tram, which proceeded smoothly up the incline. They thrust their heads out of the window and noticed big boulders lying far below them. Sum Goh murmured, "If the cable were to break …"

"We would enjoy the sensation of tumbling through space," smiled Gek Kim. They reached the terminus at the top and wandered along the paths and terraces, enjoying the cool breezes.

The area was ablaze with glorious, luxuriant flowers that diffused balmy fragrances. Sum Goh had brought his camera with him, and the first snapshot he took was of Gek Kim gazing into the distance. The town lay below, a mass of houses. No sounds from its various activities reached their ears; but to their delighted eyes it appeared a beautiful, enchanted city, washed by a soft, gleaming sea, dotted with Lilliputian vessels. The horizon was flecked with enchanting masses of clouds, the purest white.

A scene of such exquisite beauty and deep peace was bound to soothe the most agitated nerves, and Sum Goh gained a cool confidence, surprising even to himself. He felt he could perform any prodigious feat necessary, and in strong contrast to his recent growing despondency, his mind was now filled with immense joy, amounting to exultation.

After descending the hill they proceeded to the monastery at Yapi, which was visited as much for its architectural beauty as for its holy reputation. Occupying an extensive area, and built in a meandering fashion on a gentle slope, it comprised several buildings. Towering above them was a lofty pagoda, with its collection of arched roofs running round the separate storeys.

Rows of beggars in various conditions of ragged helplessness chanted their monotonous plaints as the couple trod the terraced route leading to the portal, which was guarded by two huge bronze statues with terrifying aspects. They entered the first room and became conscious of the solemn serenity pervading the place. The smell of burning incense filled the air.

A stout, flabby, shaven-headed monk came up noiselessly to them from some inner chamber and, after inquiring with admirable kindness where they came from and displaying profound interest in their welfare, concluded with a request for a subscription. The intercourse was not fruitless, and he recorded Sum Goh's name in a thick book, bowed, smiled, and retired.

They stepped reverently through various spacious halls, talking in whispers and scanning everything with due wonder. Statues of a great number of Buddhas, bodhisattvas, and arhats of various sizes made of bronze, wood, stone, or clay, some a monstrous height and others as small as dolls, appeared in every direction. Majestic forms, gleaming with gold, represented the Buddha, who once lived on earth, sitting erect and cross-legged on a lotus throne with a resplendent halo round his head, his serene, noble face absorbed in contemplation, smiling ever so mysteriously. Amitabha, the deity of the Western Paradise, was pre-eminent in importance, breathing sublime peace, compassion, and gentleness into his adherents, the most celestial in the vast assembly of figures. In one of the dim chambers was a collection of statues, representing the Eighteen Lohans arranged in rows, executed with painstaking care, altogether impressive with their magnificent decorations. In another secluded corner were two deities in martial accoutrements, Li Ching, guardian of the entrance to Heaven, and his son, No Cha, famed for his marvellous exploits. Li Ching could induce the proper degree of filial piety in his son by means of a fine miniature pagoda, which, when thrown into the air, possessed the magical power of expanding and bursting into flames around No Cha. Many ferocious demons and unfortunate spirits exuded appalling menace or the fiery anguish of unutterable punishment in Hades.

The couple walked into the courtyard, where, after the stuffiness of the rooms, the fresh air was unusually pleasant. Flowers bloomed in profusion. Two big stone pools lay at a short distance from each other. The larger one, very deep and almost dry, was filled with a vast number of tortoises, many of which crawled about a huge granite tortoise lying on the bottom and looking like the progenitor of them all. Gek Kim bought fresh green vegetables from a nearby old woman and threw them to the creatures. The other pond, which had a fountain splashing in the centre, was home to goldfish, whose bright hues gleamed through the slightly turbid water.

"Look at some of those fish," pointed Gek Kim. "Their eyes are so prominent that they seem on the point of popping out."

"Yes, it's quite curious."

They were alone; there was nobody near by. He felt it was the opportune moment for giving vent to his crucial question. He said simply, without any diffidence, "I love you, Miss Low. Will you marry me?"

She turned towards him with surprise but recovered herself quickly and then coolly uttered the staggering answer, "I will."

The answer was so unexpected that he was speechless. She looked back at the fish—they were very enchanting as they glided smoothly and noiselessly one after another, sometimes coming to the surface to breathe and then diving gracefully down again.

"I have always thought you an ideal girl," he muttered in an unsteady voice, when his astonishment had subsided sufficiently to permit him to speak.

"There is no such thing as an ideal girl. At any rate, I am not one." She smiled brightly.

"I wonder …" He hesitated.

"What makes you wonder?"

"I wonder whether you really love me."

"I shouldn't want to marry you if I didn't."

"Silly of me to ask, but I can hardly believe it."

"It is so absurd for people to marry without knowing anything of each other."

"Entirely so. You know, Miss—Gek Kim! I suppose I may call you Gek Kim now?"

"That name sounds so much more comforting."

"You know, Gek Kim, I have never been on friendly terms with any girl before."

"Not even cabaret girls?" she queried, an ironic twinkle in her dazzling eyes.

"No, never," he replied, an uncomfortable look on his face. He gazed at a stone statue, which seemed to stare back at him with a mysterious grin from its embowered seat. "Though they have become so popular."

"Don't worry! I am not jealous," declared the magnanimous Gek Kim.

"Your goodness equals your beauty."

"I asked a man I knew …"

"What?" almost shouted Sum Goh.

"What's the matter with you? Look at that sparrow resting on the right shoulder of the statue. It is preparing to fly away in terror."

"Sorry!" He looked as crestfallen as if he had lost his last dollar and was on the point of imminent starvation. "I did not mean anything whatsoever. I was just surprised, that's all. I never knew you were acquainted with any man except me."

"Don't be ridiculous! One can't help meeting men nowadays. We are no longer kept inside the house."

"But I thought that no good girl ever had much opportunity to talk with a man." Unfortunately, he was by no means as devoid of jealousy as the incomparable Gek Kim.

"If that were the case, we would never have become friends with each other at all, unless, of course, you think that I am not exactly good." She blushed with mortification and rising indignation.

"I certainly don't think anything of the sort." He was a perfect picture of contrition, induced by fear and the knowledge that he had behaved in a blameworthy manner. "Please don't be angry with me. I was a perfect fool, always have been. That's why I was surprised that you loved me at all."

All inharmonious feelings vanished from her face, which shone once more with becoming happiness.

"Fool or no fool, I have never thought twice of any man, except you. As for that particular man I was referring to, he was a friend of my father's, nearly fifty years old. He had eight wives, ranging from twenty to forty-five years old. They lived in a large house together, but not in peace. Their jealousy led them into perpetual quarrels. Not a day passed but two or more of them, and sometimes all of them, were sure to indulge in an unpleasant exchange of words or scratches. He allowed them free rein to their fancies. In fact, he enjoyed their squabbles, or at least he enjoyed relating them to my father. One day I asked him how he could stand living in an atmosphere of unceasing hostility. 'How I can stand it?' he said, his face covered with sickening glee. 'Why, I think of them as a collection of pretty cats, whose fights are highly amusing. Besides, I feel pleased to have them jealous on account of me.' I don't like to appear as a cat, even a pretty cat. Therefore I don't intend to be jealous. That does not mean, of course, that I invite you to have eight wives."

"Not even two. May thunder ..."

"Don't swear. One never knows what may happen."

"You seem to be very playful. I wish I could be as humorous about solemn matters as you are."

"Try. You'll find our life will be happier and our love ..."

"Cannot become greater, for my heart is full."

"So is mine. And now, I think it's time we go back."

That evening they announced the good news to the assembled circle of their families, who gave their hearty approval. Mrs. Lee remarked that she was extremely lucky to have such a pearl of a daughter-in-law, and Mrs. Low said, no less enthusiastically, that she had always longed for a son-in-law like Sum Goh. Their eulogies were highly embarrassing to the two young people, who were nevertheless very glad to hear them.

"We'll go back tomorrow," said Lai Pek. "There is not much more to see here. The moment we arrive home we'll begin settling all the preliminaries to the marriage."

"First," said Mrs. Lee, "there is the comparison of their horoscopes to see whether these agree with each other. There is the well-known diviner ..."

"I dare say they will be in perfect harmony," stated Lai Pek with conviction. "Of course, there must be a formal engagement as soon as possible. When do you wish the marriage to take place, Mr. Low?"

"I think we should choose an auspicious day somewhere towards the end of the year. It will be only a few months hence."

"Good! That's settled."

While all these delightful plans on their behalf were under discussion, the couple, who were going to be the principal performers in the drama, offered no suggestions of their own, nor were their opinions solicited. They smiled in acquiescence, not caring very much what ceremonies they had to undergo as long as they were united in matrimony. Gek Kim thought that it was best to let her elders have their way in the arrangements, for she did not want to begrudge them their share of happiness in the event.

"Of course," said Mrs. Lee, after a pause in the conversation, "we must get hold of a go-between. In this case there is really none, but one would be necessary in connection with the ceremonies. We'll request Mrs. Ka Soh's services. She is very popular in that capacity."

"As you wish," said Mrs. Low in gracious assent.

"We'll have the most glorious wedding Lanta has ever seen," continued Mrs. Lee, with appropriate pride. "A wedding that will make the town stare in wonder and draw crowds from the villages—a wedding such as, unfortunately, we never had, for your father, Sum Goh, was very miserly in those days."

"If I had not been very thrifty when I was younger, you would not be able to talk now of our family being able to afford a glorious wedding," retorted Lai Pek. "You see, Sum Goh, I had only just begun to earn a little. I had to make my way in the world. When I reached manhood, I had no father to provide a handsome wedding for me. I had to find the money myself. Of course, we did not marry through our own choice. My uncle chose the bride. But he defrayed only a part of the expenses."

What a lamentable topic, thought Sum Goh, *such lack of taste to refer to these by-no-means dignified facts.* He had never heard his father allude to his early struggles before, and he liked to think they had always been tolerably well off. His father had all the satisfaction of a self-made man; he wanted to bathe in the lake of hereditary prestige.

But Gek Kim was all sympathy and interest. "You must feel, Uncle Lee, great pleasure in your achievements." She would have to change her title of addressing him when she was married to his son, but at present she still called him by the polite term. "It's always better to do something than to inherit something."

"You are a very sensible girl," declared Lai Pek. "I am proud of you." He glanced round, impressed, to indicate that his pride was genuine; it, of course, afforded the highest gratification to Gek Kim, or should have, at any rate. "The well-expressed maxim says, 'Under Heaven none has succeeded without toil.' I have always tried to follow it," he added complacently.

"About the day of marriage," said Mrs. Low, "I don't know whether there will be sufficient time for all the necessary preparations to be made."

"Why, what's up?" asked Mrs. Lee.

"For one thing, Gek Kim has never learned to make any embroidered slippers. You know, a girl should, if possible, embroider thirty or forty pairs herself, which on her marriage can be distributed to the relatives and best friends of both the families of the bride and bridegroom. Gek Kim hasn't a single pair."

Gek Kim looked rather guilty, as if to confirm the statement.

"Fortunately," said Mrs. Lee, "this custom is no longer essential. You can buy them if you want them as presents."

"But no one makes them ready for sale."

"We can commission a few people to start making them. And if not enough can be made in time, a few will do equally well."

"And then there are so many things to do." Mrs. Low was rather a fussy, methodical person, who paid great attention to details and needed plenty of time in which to do any task. "We have to engage the master of ceremonies, gather the bridesmaids and bridegroom's attendants, make so many dresses …"

"All these things can be done in a very short period," stated the efficient Lai Pek.

It must be confessed that during the latter part of their respectable parents' discourse, Sum Goh and Gek Kim were carrying on a private conversation between themselves, which they might have found very entertaining but which they had no business to conduct in almost a whisper for their exclusive benefit. It was highly disrespectful to their seniors; they should have known better and paid silent attention to what was being said. Gek Kim seemed to be relating some amusing anecdote, for her dark eyes were bright with merriment, delicious smiles rippled over her warm face, and her bare arms were stretched straight in front of her, apparently to illustrate some particular point.

"Well," remarked Tua Sai with a careless yawn, indicative of his easy-going disposition, "I must confess I am not much interested in details concerning marriage requirements.

Neither are the two on whose account this discussion has arisen."

They all laughed heartily as they glanced at those two, who started and looked confused, not knowing what the others were laughing about, only knowing from the direction of their eyes that they were feeling amused at their expense.

Chapter 13

The Tiger's Attack

Never was there a more beautiful estate in the country than his, Lai Pek was fond of telling various people, who in his presence smiled in polite assent but in his absence made unflattering remarks. The rubber trees were marvellously productive, too, being mature, juicy trees, and the latex collected was peculiarly abundant. He paid great attention to the estate's proper upkeep, inspected it at regular intervals of a few days and gave instructions to the overseer to be certain the tappers did not spoil the trees and produced spotless sheets of smoked rubber. The income he derived was satisfactory, as the product commanded a high price. There was no sign that this high level would not be maintained; in fact, prices showed a decided tendency to rise to even greater heights. He was glad he had bought the estate at a reasonable bargain from the hard-up owner and never failed to congratulate himself on his wisdom in making such a lucrative investment. It seemed improbable he would ever wish to part with it or would ever regard it with anything but affection. He began to indulge in dreams.

"I do not intend to spend the income from the estate," he told Hwey Pin. "I am going to use it, together with any additional money I may be able to save from my business, in buying additional acres. I have seen strips of good land surrounding mine. Do you think the owners would be willing to sell them?"

"I dare say they would, if a good price were offered," replied Hwey Pin, rapidly calculating the amount of commission he should ask for in future. His mental arithmetic released a glorious fount of satisfaction in his mind and made him grin, revealing a missing incisor in his lower jaw. "Luckily they are under different persons, who own only a few acres each."

"What a glorious thing rubber is! It's a pity I wasn't connected with it earlier."

"You'll soon be a vast landed proprietor," said Hwey Pin in a profoundly convinced tone.

Lai Pek smiled but offered no reply, as to express agreement would be to deviate from the convention of assuming becoming modesty. On the other hand, he sincerely believed the statement; therefore, the best course was to offer a slightly disparaging look and remain silent.

He strolled to the door of his shop and gazed out. Although it was only nine o'clock in the morning, it was uncomfortably hot, and the sun was rapidly increasing the intensity of its rays. Enormous masses of picturesque white clouds—fold on shining fold, floating about elfishly—decorated the heavens. It was the hot season of the year, and no rain had fallen for weeks.

Amid jostling confusion people were hurrying to and fro, busy as ever. The thought came into his mind that he was much superior to the crowd, especially in sagacity. Everything that he touched yielded him profit—the question with him was not, as with others, whether his enterprises entailed gain or loss, but whether they were highly or (contemptible thing!) only ordinarily profitable. Take this investment—if he became owner of many acres of excellent land, he might even retire from business, in which he had toiled quite long enough. If the estate continued to be prosperous, as it undoubtedly would, he would be able to increase its area. But had he been aware of what had happened that very morning, it was unlikely he would have dreamed thus.

About a dozen tappers worked laboriously on the estate and were given enough wages to prevent them from making a speedy departure to the nether regions. Some were contented; others were chiefly concerned about their daily quota of opium and derived their highest bliss when they lay beside their pipes and lamps, stinting themselves of food to that end. Some fretted but had to stick to their jobs for want of a better option. Among them was a young man of strong physique who still preserved some of his joy in life, though there was little to gladden him; his chief amusement was to recite ballads and play a flute in the evening with a vast amount of enthusiasm. The routine of his life was simple: he rose at four every morning and headed out with a tapping knife and a can to hold the sap. The labourers dispersed to various parts of the land. He would return with his day's produce at about nine o'clock and undergo a further spell of work at the shed where the rubber was treated. He was practically free in the afternoons, so he would often take a walk to the neighbouring town and spend the time in pleasant conversation with some friends.

On the particular day in question, which saw Lai Pek indulging in complacent speculations about the acquisition of fresh land, the unfortunate tapper rose very early, as usual. The dawn was cool and invigorating. *How good it is just to breathe,* he thought as he trod among the fallen leaves. The trees that fell to his lot to tap occupied ground bordering the forest. As he set to work with a will, the sun was still below the horizon, but rosy light suffused the eastern sky.

He heard the crack of a twig behind him, and he turned round to see a tiger of more than ordinary size approaching him. He stood and faced it, too paralysed to move; there was no time to climb a tree, even if his limbs had not temporarily refused to stir. The tiger gazed at him, gave a horrible cough, and shook in anger, looking a picture of vengeance, its flaming hide streaked with black. The man suddenly came to life and stirred, emitting a loud cry for help. At that moment the beast roared and leapt. The man sprang to the right, and before it could turn, seized hold of the tiger's tail, for he laboured under a curious belief that the best way to cope with a tiger was to grasp its tail firmly and prevent it from coming face to face with him by continually dodging behind its back. There was only a very short time, however, that the brute could not get at him; it suddenly swung round with such force that he fell down. It struck a vicious paw and removed his lower jaw. He was knocked senseless and, in a short interval, half his body had passed piece by gory piece through the huge, growling cavern of the tiger's mouth.

The other tappers, who were far away, separated by dense rows of intervening trees, did not see the attack, but those nearest the scene heard the brute's roars. Dropping their knives in astonishment and terror, they ran and, though they could not distinguish from which direction the sounds actually came, three of them by chance found themselves close to the place on their way back to their huts. The terrible spectacle made them shout with all their might, causing the beast to look up with dripping jaws. One, acting with greater presence of mind, hurled a large knife that he usually carried in his belt, and, as luck would direct, it entered the beast's yawning mouth, cutting its tongue. After hesitating for a brief second, as if contemplating revenge, the beast quickly turned and slinked back into the jungle.

Soon the entire staff of the estate collected round the mangled body. Consternation and horror blanched every face, and nameless dread seared a path through every heart. They were not unfamiliar with the faint growls of distant beasts, but that one of their peers should have suffered such an agonizing fate was too awful. The dead man had no relatives and was extremely well liked by those who knew him; the women wept and wailed in sympathy and terror.

"What an untimely death!" said one man.

"The God of Hades has called him away," said a second.

"The sooner one dies, the less trouble one meets," said a third.

"It's one thing to die safe in bed with weeping relatives around and another thing to meet such a violent end," said a fourth.

"Fate is fate," declared a solemn man. "He was telling me only yesterday that he was going to quit this job next week and work for a bicycle repairer in town. He said that when he had saved something he would set up shop for himself. In fact, never did he seem happier. And now ..."

"This estate is unblessed," said a man with only one ear. "We should never have come here."

They all looked at one another; the same thought flashed through each mind like a streak of lightning.

"I wonder when the tiger will come back and whom it will meet the next time?" continued the one-eared man.

"Don't utter such unlucky words," grumbled the solemn man.

"Once a tiger has tasted human flesh, it will hunger for it and is sure to come prowling about its old neighbourhood," continued the one-eared man, disregarding the interruption.

Suddenly a woman gave a scream, ghastly in its emotional intensity.

"Ghost!" she exclaimed, one finger rigidly pointing towards the corpse.

They all involuntarily retreated a step.

"I thought I saw the body move," she explained tearfully.

"What a parcel of silly people you are!" exclaimed the overseer, who hitherto had not paid any attention to their conversation, being absorbed in his own sad reflections and considering what he ought to do.

"After all," said the one-eared man, "there is no reason why the ghost of the poor deceased should not appear. The ghosts of people who die violent deaths are always particularly ferocious."

Cold sweat moistened the pale faces of the shaking spectators.

"I am leaving the estate," declared the one-eared man decisively. "If we delay till trouble really comes upon us, then, as is commonly said, 'if one wants to ascend the sky, it has no road; to dive into the earth, it has no gate.' We would be extremely foolish to linger here a moment longer."

He broke into a run in the direction of his hut, and the others followed his inspired example.

"Come back!" shouted the overseer. "Even if his ghost haunted this place, it would not injure you. You were always on friendly terms with the man when he was alive."

"Ghosts that haunt the earth have been known to do curious things," one roared as he ran. "Besides, even if the ghost doesn't appear, the tiger will."

On reaching their huts, they hastily packed their meagre belongings in blankets, and, swinging the bundles over their shoulders, they departed without more ado. Fortunately for them, they had received their month's wages only the previous day, so there remained nothing to detain them a moment longer. The overseer found himself, except for his family, alone on that piece of unhallowed land. He informed the police about the tragedy, and when they had removed the remnants of the body and all the necessary particulars had been noted, he came to Lanta to apprise his employer of the details.

It must be admitted that, as he received the shocking news on his doorstep that hot morning, Lai Pek felt some sympathy for his dead employee, though he had hardly ever seen him and could not quite recollect what he was like. He was constitutionally averse to such violent tragedies; he did not wish them to happen, even to his enemies. But, to tell the truth, he felt sorrier for himself as he sat behind his counter under an unparalleled gloom.

"The idiots! The cowards!" he exclaimed angrily. "To abscond in a group in that heartless way! The ungrateful wretches!" What they had to be grateful for he did not explicitly reveal; perhaps because he kept them alive through the wages he gave in exchange for their work.

"Very obstinate people," said the overseer. "I could not persuade them to stay."

"You should have restrained them by force," retorted Lai Pek heatedly, for he had lost his usual bland serenity.

The overseer's eyes bulged in wonder and threatened to remain in that state forever.

"Oh! I am ruined!" moaned Lai Pek with an unwonted lack of dignity. "It is impossible to engage fresh hands for months to come, perhaps for years—perhaps forever. No man will dare to live on the estate now."

"It may not be as bad as that. Some workers may be induced to stay with especially high wages," said Hwey Pin.

"And I get no profit whatsoever, of course," snapped Lai Pek truculently. "I was a fool to listen to your advice about buying that piece of land. Why didn't you tell me that there were tigers prowling about?"

Hwey Pin was a patient man, and he made due allowances for his friend's well-nigh demented state. "How could I know that tigers were to be found there? None had appeared during the previous owner's occupation."

"This means that Heaven wishes to punish me for some unknown reason. I'll never buy another estate. What a curse rubber is!" He flatly contradicted the opinion he had expressed not half an hour before. "I only wish I could sell this detestable one. But I don't think any fool will ever want to buy it and ruin himself as a result."

Hwey Pin shook his head in compassion but thought it best to remain silent. For several days Lai Pek consistently refused to open his mouth to utter more than a few words and in fact shut himself up in his room, temporarily abandoning his shop to the somewhat precarious control of his clerk—precarious indeed, for he could not be expected to exercise that ardent enthusiasm and unwearying devotion so indispensable to commercial success.

Chapter 14

A Legal Contest

The rivalry between Lai Pek and Beng Hu dragged on without any visible advantage on either side, as their cakes were both equally popular. In spite of the low prices, which severe competition had forced on them, they contrived to realise some profit, owing to the enormous sales; but this state of affairs was by no means satisfactory to either party.

With regard to their personal relationship, they had never communicated much with each other. Except when they were inadvertently brought face to face, as sometimes happened, then having to utter some meaningless phrases of courteous greeting, they could hardly bring themselves to pass remarks upon the slightest topics, while they scrupulously avoided making any reference to trade. If they chanced to meet in the club, they immediately entered different rooms and joined different groups of people. If one was passing along a road and saw the other coming from a distance, he found that his most convenient route lay in a different direction.

Once, when Lai Pek was taking a leisurely walk through a busy thoroughfare, he saw Beng Hu approaching him. On a stretch of sandy ground by the side of the road, a juggler was entertaining a cheering crowd of mostly ragged customers with prodigious feats of magic, performing a host of unbelievable stunts. He swallowed a mass of coloured shreds of paper with every evidence of enjoyment and then proceeded to pull from his mouth a long string of the same material, which on emergence he twined into a ball. He showed the audience an empty tin pot whose inside was perfectly dry, placed it on the sand, and covered it with a dirty piece of cloth. Then he burnt a small paper image; after an interval he whisked away the cloth, and lo! the pot was full of rice wine. The juggler had secretly conveyed it from some unlucky wine merchant: to provc that it was genuine alcoholic liquor, he poured it down the throats of two old men from among the bystanders, who drank it avidly, smacked their lips, and exclaimed excitedly that it was what it was supposed to be.

Lai Pek scarcely stood for even a quarter of an hour to watch such exhibitions, as he considered it undignified to join the vulgar mob but, in order to avoid Beng Hu, he squeezed his way into the ring of spectators. The performer went round the circle once, striking a gong; then he began to juggle four stout wooden bars, throwing two into the air while retaining only one in either hand at a time. Faster and faster flew the pieces and subtler became the movements; they were thrown from behind him and passed through his legs. When the excitement was at its peak, one of the bars eluded his clutch and swept past Lai Pek, striking his nose, which bled under the force of the impact. The disagreeable ragamuffins screamed with merriment, and Lai Pek made a hasty retreat, chagrined. He, strangely enough, imputed his mishap to Beng Hu, thus creating a new grievance against him.

Hwey Pin approached him with another proposition to injure his rival's atrocious prosperity. "Our contest will never come to a decisive end till we ruin him by a bold trick," he said unctuously.

"What bold trick?" asked Lai Pek with obvious distaste, for since the affair of the estate he was not disposed to heed Hwey Pin's suggestions; besides, the word *trick* was not connotative of the superior wisdom Lai Pek claimed but of low cunning, which he disliked.

"His product seems to be equally popular with ours. To make it unpopular, we should secretly turn out yam cakes bearing his chop, to all appearance the same as his, but bitter, with an atrocious taste. After a few tins are sold, people will avoid his stuff like dung."

"This is monstrous!" exclaimed Lai Pek. "It's forgery. We could go to prison for it."

"I don't see what's monstrous about it," responded Hwey Pin coldly. "Everything is fair in competition. And as for going to prison, who is to know about our deception, if we work skilfully?"

"I am not going to join this conspiracy."

A vision of Beng Hu's triumphant prosperity and his own miserable defeat rose in Lai Pek's mind; he recoiled from it in disgust and accepted the proposal, the recollection of his bleeding nose materially assisting his decision.

A fortnight later people began to spit out yam cake in horror, for the nauseating taste of the first bite would not vanish, even after a whole jug of water. When a customer bought a tin, he or she was not certain whether it would contain the usual delicacy or poison. The rumour spread that Beng Hu had a mad employee who was a mass murderer and had conceived this subtle plan to get rid of the population wholesale. Some irresponsible persons even went so far as to suggest that Beng Hu himself, bloated with conceit at his tremendous success, was deliberately trying to insult the townsfolk, imagining that anything bearing his logo must please, so great was his prestige; but that ridiculous suggestion was not given general credence. In any case, the yam cakes absolutely ceased to sell, and Lai Pek was left in sole possession of the field, making profits, which somewhat soothed his conscience.

Beng Hu's grief on discovering this horrible calamity was immense, and indignation coiled round his heart with the tenacity of a boa constrictor. After carefully supervising his shop and scrutinising the products issued, he came to the only conclusion possible under the circumstances—no one, savc his rival, could have any motive in perpetrating such a hoax. For an infinitesimal instant he thought of retaliating in the same manner, but feeling ashamed, he dismissed the idea. If his opponents chose to wallow in slime, there was no reason why he should dip his hand into the same substance.

Fearing that the unhappy effect on his business might endure forever, he decided it was time to take drastic steps. First, however, he would approach Lai Pek to try to address the matter.

He found the latter was ensconced behind his counter, feeling a little depressed over his idle estate, for which he had conceived an aversion commensurate with his former admiration. Beng Hu had already crossed the threshold before Lai Pek looked up and encountered his gaze; otherwise, he could easily have disappeared behind the partition and avoided his presence, but Lai Pek could not very well do so now with any appearance of propriety.

They smiled, very faintly, and muttered some incoherent words.

"I have come here, Mr. Lee," stated Beng Hu, without beating about the bush, "on a matter of some importance to both of us."

"Only important matters ever interest me," replied Lai Pek ponderously, as he stared at his diligent clerk at the other end of the room, who was rapidly writing grass characters in a ledger with a hair brush, held perpendicularly.

"This unfortunate competition between our shops with respect to cakes is most distressing."

"Very regrettable indeed," murmured Lai Pek.

"Can't we put a stop to it?"

"That's a problem," replied Lai Pek suavely, "which has been engaging my attention for some time."

"We could fix a stable price, which should leave us a reasonable margin of profit, much more than either of us made during the last few months."

"That is a proposition which I shall lay before my partners as soon as possible."

"As for the bogus cakes issued under my chop, which have done so much injury to my purse and reputation …"

"I am glad to hear you did not manufacture those," smiled Lai Pek, glancing at his clerk, now engaged in complicated arithmetical calculations upon an abacus, which produced a pleasant succession of sounds as the balls struck one another. "There are rumours that they came from your place."

"Who would be so silly as to do something to destroy himself?" demanded Beng Hu, with a perceptible flush on his cheeks. The iron bands of ceremony were getting too tight.

"True! True!" exclaimed Lai Pek swiftly. "Who could have palmed off that stuff as yours?"

"I think there is only one company that could have any interest in such an artifice," said Beng Hu, recovering his composure.

"I am afraid I'm unable to follow your allusion," responded Lai Pek coldly.

"I think you can—or else your manager can."

"If you are under the impression that the company of which I am only a partner, although the chief, could ever condescend to such a trick, you are mistaken."

"Then that company will not cease making that hideous stuff?"

"That company has never had anything to do with it. As a matter of fact, your absurd suspicions reflect on our honesty. If they were not so ridiculous and my partners such peaceful men and respectable inhabitants of this town for decades, we would sue you for libel."

"When I came, I expected we would reach a happy agreement."

"And I never bargained for a brutal insult, unprecedented in the history of my humble life."

"I am going to bring the case before a court of law."

"If you have a case at all and can find no better way of squandering your money, I entreat you to do so."

Beng Hu retired; bland politeness reigned. Not one of the functionaries in the shop could have known that they had just witnessed what amounted to a bitter quarrel. Beng Hu forthwith set about putting his threat into action. The first necessity was evidently to seek legal advice. For this purpose he took a trip to Napi, a town larger than Lanta and about sixty miles away. The court, to which more important cases were relegated, was located there, and a thriving number of lawyers' firms were within a stone's throw of its fine edifice.

Beng Hu alighted at the large, domed railway station with a bag in his hand. Ten minutes later he found himself in Padang Road, scrutinising an oblong copper plate, on which were inscribed in glaring letters the words, Messrs. Lek and Ooi, Advocates and Solicitors. Walking up a narrow flight of steps, he entered a bustling office.

"May I see either Mr. Lek or Mr. Ooi?" inquired Beng Hu of the chief clerk, who at the time was gazing at the wall with an abstraction worthy of a monk wrapped in holy meditation.

"What! Pardon me," said the clerk, recalled to mundane affairs. "I am afraid I did not catch what you were saying."

Beng Hu repeated his question.

"Mr. Ooi is at court, but Mr. Lek will see you as soon as he has finished an interview with a client."

That client soon emerged with a face bedewed with tears, a pathetic picture of helplessness as she walked out with her eyes bent on the ground. The chief clerk languidly signalled to a minion to usher Beng Hu into the chamber of Mr. Lek, who glanced at the visitor with a smile of welcome, which quickly gave place to a professional air of attention. He looked approximately fifty years of age and was quite bald at the top of his head. His height might have been five foot one without hat or shoes, and he wore a complete set of artificial teeth. He was urbane and jovial with his clients but portentous to his adversaries.

"I wish to consult you upon an affair connected with trade," began Beng Hu in a cool, deliberate manner.

"Trade at present," said Mr. Lek, "is in a satisfactory state of prosperity."

"No doubt. But mine has been injured by an unscrupulous fraud. I wish to sue its perpetrators."

Mr. Lek was extremely peculiar as a lawyer. "Wait—before we proceed further, can you assure me that you are in the right?" he asked. "I never defend a person who has evidently done wrong."

"If there is a case that is absolutely good in the moral sense, it is the one I am bringing you. I dislike evil as much as you do."

"On such a basis, I shall be glad to act for you. Please proceed with your story."

Beng Hu unfolded the whole history of his enterprises from the day he settled in Lanta to his last interview with Lai Pek.

"I see," said Mr. Lek, after listening to the discourse with exemplary patience. "I may say that your enemies' actions were prompted by envy and malice."

"That is as clear as the sun."

"You are most unfortunate to have settled in such a town. But, after all, no matter where you choose to carry on your business, you will probably meet with opposition. There are always people to be found who envy the prosperity of others."

"What do you think of my case?" asked Beng Hu, coming to the real point at issue.

"Yours is a very fine case. There is no doubt we shall win. But at present we have very little evidence to prove that the imitation product comes from them."

"No one else could have any motive in producing it."

"True, but that is not direct evidence."

"Do you mean to say we have to wait till we catch them in the act?"

"Not necessarily. I'll tell you what we'll do. You'll entice one of their workers to enter your service with higher wages, say. Get one who knows the secret of the affair. He will stand as witness and he will be able to give us valuable information."

"That is rather a difficult thing to do," responded Beng Hu, not relishing this underhanded procedure.

"Very easy," said Mr. Lek. "In any case, this is the best method for absolutely defeating your enemies."

As he could not think of any acceptable alternative, Beng Hu agreed to the suggestion. "As for your fees …"

"That point," stated the lawyer, displaying his false teeth and looking as if he had now come down to real business, "is easily settled."

Leaving the premises of Messrs. Lek and Ooi, Beng Hu skirted the bank of a shallow river that ran through the middle of the town, lost in profound reflection about the undignified struggle into which he had entered. He vaguely wondered when it would end.

Two days afterwards he succeeded in inducing an employee of the Avenging Lion to transfer his services to him in consideration of a sum of fifty dollars down and higher wages, five dollars per month in excess of what he had been receiving. The man asserted he knew everything about the deception and was prepared to swear to the truth of his revelations any time. It seemed that Hwey Pin had consistently treated him with unwarranted contempt, having always called him, not by his name or any respectable mode of address, but by the unlovely monosyllable *eh*, as though he were a dog, and he would have left him in any case. Soon afterwards the company, of which Lai Pek was the main pillar, received a notification from the court that they were called upon to defend a case brought against them by Sin Beng Hu, plaintiff.

Hwey Pin was the guiding spirit in the energetic defence. Their cause was ably advocated by Mr. Uan of Messrs. Tit and Uan, whose firm was separated from that of Messrs. Lek and Ooi by a wall. The contest that ensued rocked Lanta like a storm; the case looked as if it would be rather prolonged, however, and whether it would ultimately benefit the litigants or not, it certainly was not prejudicial to the pockets of their lawyers, for sand flies when two rocks collide.

Chapter 15

Gek Kim's Disappearance

The cheap lodging house, with the stupendous mass of humanity thronging its cramped space and its proximity to the market, provided an exquisite abode for a person whose ears appreciated tumultuous noise. Conversation was a stimulating exercise of the vocal cords, and parsimony in the use of words was assuredly not one of the outstanding vices of the residents. Their feet demanded and obtained their due share of the privilege of producing sound; beneath heavy wooden clogs and forceful bare feet, the floors thudded and the rickety stairs creaked. The lodgers were not particularly fastidious; everyone who felt the inclination, which was uncommonly strong, expectorated anywhere they pleased. Refuse of all sorts, from matchboxes and torn sheets of paper to durian husks and bones, formed a carpet; and the exotic mixture of smells pervading the atmosphere, though of suspect bouquet, was nevertheless such a persistent phenomenon that it did not attract any attention.

Under its protective roof, where a bed was available at a very low rate, each canvas bed separated from the next by a space of one foot, was gathered a motley multitude of patrons: rickshaw pullers, hawkers, stall keepers, shop assistants, vegetable gardeners, mining coolies and a whole host of fortune tellers, acrobats, vendors of quack panaceas, and others who gained a subsistence along the sides of streets. They came, stayed for days or weeks, finished whatever business had brought them, and departed. But during their short acquaintances lodgers were very sociable and communicative, and strangers easily fell into conversation, with no need for any introduction. Despite their unkempt appearance, many possessed a fathomless fund of cheerfulness, produced not by external circumstances, over which they had no control, but by an inborn antipathy towards solemnity.

A popular personality, ever ready to enter into a confidential chat, was a pedlar whose left hand, instead of the customary five, was tipped with six fingers, the extra one, next to the little finger and about half as long, though clearly superfluous and useless, still serving as an ornamental appendage. Though not at all merry, he still loved to indulge in free and easy discourse, which procured him ready sympathy. Evidently a widely travelled and observant man, he could relate a fine variety of anecdotes, which bore a flavour of romantic adventure and whose influence on the humdrum lives of his audience was stimulating. He had been in the house less than a week. His trade, that of an itinerant pedlar, was to travel through towns and villages selling feather brushes, needles, towels, knives, and other small articles, which he carried in two light boxes, slung across his shoulders at the end of a wooden pole. He was out during a great part of the day hawking his wares, but he was not usually absent at night, except for brief hours.

He spent long periods of time trying to extract information about the town and its principal men of wealth from the landlord, who saw nothing unusual in the queries and was only too proud and pleased to impart whatever he knew, chiefly from hearsay and embellished by his own inventions. The result of his investigations from this and other sources was that he became particularly interested in the house of Low Tua Sai and frequently found occasion to pass it in his capacity as a pedlar. He had a distinct bias for the company of a woodcutter, who was also a lodger, having arrived the day after him, and who went about with an axe, chopping thick pieces of firewood into more handy forms for those who engaged him for such tasks, thus procuring an intimate knowledge of kitchens that encouraged gossiping with domestic servants. The two men were often seen together, and it was supposed that their sudden intimacy was due to their common roots in one clan; they spoke between themselves in a mysterious dialect unknown to their fellow lodgers.

On the sixth morning of his residence in the town, the pedlar was in front of Low Tua Sai's house, selling needles to a maidservant, who found an immense pleasure in handling all his merchandise and making inquiries as to prices, even though she had no intention of being a purchaser. But he was genial and tolerant and enjoyed her innocent prattle with great gusto, while he casually dropped questions relating to domestic affairs.

Gek Kim and Sum Goh appeared, obviously going somewhere for a visit, and as they passed by, Gek Kim told the servant that, when her father or mother returned, she was to say they were gone to the hot water spring. They then stepped into a car and drove off.

"An elegant lady," remarked the pedlar nonchalantly, by way of polite conversation. "The daughter of your master, I suppose?"

"Yes," asserted the servant, turning over and over a piece of red ribbon. "This looks nice."

"Undoubtedly," said the pedlar carelessly. "The hot water spring. Is that the one about fifteen miles from here?"

"I suppose so. I know of no other around about these parts," replied the servant. "I'll take this ribbon."

"Very good. It will look nice around your hair," said the pedlar, packing his wares into their proper places. "And now, if you want nothing more, I shall be going."

The pedlar walked leisurely away, but once out of sight of the bungalow, he made quick progress towards the lodging house. Immediately thereafter, he and the woodcutter settled their bills, hired a car, and alighted at a spot nearly a hundred yards from the gate, by the side of the road that led to the spring and disappeared into an estate.

Sum Goh and Gek Kim stood on the brim of an extensive shallow pool, watching the warm water ceaselessly bubbling through the bed. Similar pools lay around, the issuing water flowing into streams. The landscape was suffused with a certain wild charm, and except for a few habitations and occasional visitors, imparted a desolate grandeur. In the distance cascades tumbled down steep slopes, the glistening spray bathed in sunlight.

After gazing at the pools with great interest for some time, Sum Goh and Gek Kim wandered around the place, among the tall trees. They sat down in a shady spot.

"I'll go and see if I can get some drinks," said Sum Goh to Gek Kim; he walked briskly towards a hut that lay some distance away, concealed from view. The pedlar and the woodcutter, who had followed them from town and had been secretly watching their movements, were now treading like panthers within a thicket close behind Gek Kim. They suddenly darted out, and before she became aware of their presence, a hand was clapped over her mouth, to be swiftly followed by a strong gag; then together they carried her back to the spot where they had emerged. With some difficulty owing to her struggles, which, though undeniably valiant, were of no avail against the united strength of two men, they hurried her along without regard to her comfort and soon entered a forest.

"Come now," said the former pedlar, drawing from his pocket an unprepossessing little pistol and pointing it for an unpleasant moment at Gek Kim. "Move rapidly, and don't try to run away. This instrument can behave disastrously."

After they had penetrated a considerable depth into the jungle, the pedlar—for so he must still be identified, though he was without his boxes, and his conduct was strange for that of a member of that peaceful and honourable occupation—removed the gag from her mouth.

"Don't try to shout for help," he admonished. "No one will hear you. In any case, as young ladies should always speak with soft voices, I wish you to maintain that modest behaviour, even if I have to use my pistol."

"What is the meaning of this outrageous treatment?" demanded Gek Kim angrily when she found that she was able to speak.

"Don't get excited, little sister," soothed the pedlar, "you are in no real danger."

"But why have you brought me here?"

"Just a matter of business. We intend to restore you to your father, safe and sound, in exchange for a trifling sum of money, which is important to us poor wretches but doubtless perfectly superfluous to him."

"Kidnapped!" exclaimed Gek Kim. "You are robbers?"

"That word bears an ugly meaning. I object to your use of it, especially in that uncomplimentary tone. Our benevolent object is to relieve the rich of their troublesome money."

Gek Kim had by this time recovered her usual charming coolness, and she realised that, for the present at any rate, she had no option but to accept the inevitable and follow them to their unsavoury retreat. The forest through which they were travelling was quite dry and did not look wild enough to harbour any dangerous animals. There were no well-marked paths, but her captors propelled her along without any hesitation.

"Doubtless you think ill of us," remarked the pedlar. "But we must make a living, you know."

"What kind of a living do you call this?" demanded Gek Kim, shaken out of her equanimity for a moment. "Kidnapping innocent people and plundering houses!"

"Every man has his own choice of a profession," said the brigand, perfectly free from any shadow of embarrassment. "Some want to be doctors, lawyers, merchants, jugglers; I love mine."

"I dare say you do."

"There is another reason why I stick to my work. If I were to become a supposedly respectable person, I would just be a miserable coolie, earning a trifling sum a day and despised by everybody to boot. Not a very comforting prospect."

"Do you think that ill-gotten wealth can atone for a troubled conscience?"

"It would certainly be a curse, provided one has a conscience. Luckily, I have long ago banished mine."

Gek Kim stared at him in unmitigated horror, but he did not resent the impression he produced.

"Are you the leader of a band of…"

"Don't use that undignified word. I am not. I am only the second in command. Our leader is a young man of forceful personality."

If her nerves had not been under perfect control, Gek Kim might have collapsed in shocked amazement. As it was, her brain reeled for a moment, but except for a slight start that was not noticed by the robbers, she gave no outward indication of her mental state. Her abduction might turn out more seriously than she had hitherto imagined, might become more than a mere question of ransom. She dared not allow her imagination to run over all the possible consequences, but she was certain of one thing—she must keep her wits about her.

"You are extraordinarily cool for a young lady in your circumstances, though," observed the other robber, who had posed as a woodcutter and whose torn, soiled shirt and shorts still smelled of damp firewood. He was a minor member of his band and had hitherto remained silent. "Most girls scream and cry even when they are only aware that we are inside their houses and haven't seen us yet."

"She is undoubtedly brave," said the pedlar. "I admire your deportment, little sister."

"Why should I be afraid of you?" retorted Gek Kim, her heart quaking a little nevertheless. "I have never feared anything."

"Indeed!" laughed the pedlar. "If so, you are better than many a man. I hope you keep up your character. Tears never affect us with sympathy, and they are extremely annoying. Don't resort to them. You will go home in good time, none the worse for your adventure, I assure you."

CHAPTER 16

In thc Cave

They reached a hill, up whose slope the forest climbed, spreading its network of trees among great overhanging rocks. The wild, desolate scene was impressive in its rugged majesty, and it embraced a hint of subtle mystery, intensified by the modest light that filtered through the canopy. Many caves of indeterminate size, with jagged, irregularly shaped edges, penetrated the base of the hill. It looked as though hordes of ferocious beasts crawled within their confines and might rush unwelcomingly towards anyone who dared to approach the vicinity. Gek Kim looked with disfavour around her; as they stood at the mouth of a cave, conveniently concealed from casual scrutiny behind a clump of bushes, she asked the pedlar, with evident disapproval in her tone, whether they resided there.

"Certainly," replied the man, rather nettled. "What's the matter with it?"

They passed through a dim passage, made several devious turns, and arrived at a hole of indescribable shape, which the pedlar called the anteroom. He vanished through another opening for an instant, and the woodcutter turned into a corridor on the right, leaving her in the company of a most disagreeable-looking person with a crooked mouth, who was gobbling a huge bowl of congee. Crooked Mouth looked up for an instant, gazed at her in wonder, grinned a curious specimen of a grin, a variety she had never seen before, then bent his head over his dish and went on with his meal. The pedlar soon emerged and ushered her into a compartment, which had some semblance of a furnished room, as it was adorned with a small table at one end, together with a couple of wooden chairs and a wooden bed. It was more or less oblong in shape and did not look forbidding. Though the light was dim, it was sufficient to permit a reasonable degree of visibility.

The pedlar withdrew, and she found herself face to face with the chief of the band, who, clad in a dark shirt and trousers to match, sat grimly at the table. They gazed at each other in the gloomy chamber, and as she approached him, her look of hostility changed to one of incredulity, which was reflected to almost as great an extent on his countenance. Dismay swept across her brow, for she was in the presence of her lost cousin, he who could not wean himself from an inglorious habit and to whom was imputed a crime that had sadly tarnished the name of his family. By what twist of fate had he come to occupy his monstrous position? She could only gaze in dumb astonishment. In spite of a certain change—for one thing, he was older—his appearance retained the same essential traits: the thick mass of black hair, parted in the centre, the daring, speculative attitude of a gambler pursued by a relentless fate to risk everything in the hope of success—all these were still conspicuously discernible. But something else was also clearly identifiable—the authoritative demeanour of one whose will was law.

He was the first to recover from his surprise. "You are the person whom they caught?" he remarked, sternly but not unkindly.

"Yes, I am that luckless person," she responded, in a tone that indicated an attempt at gentleness, but unfortunately the desire outran the achievement. Even though he was a robber, she still could not bring herself to hate him as he deserved. She remembered her aunt, who had died because of him, and she had always felt a strange sympathy for him, believing him to be the victim of hapless fate.

"They mentioned a girl, but I never thought it was you."

"I thought you were the leader."

"I am," he remarked proudly.

"Then you must have arranged everything."

"As it so happened, I didn't. I sent my assistant to survey the town, but I did not tell him to capture anyone in particular. Of course, being my most trusted man, I allowed him a certain freedom to do as he thought fit."

"I suppose you knew that we lived there."

"To tell you the truth, I did not think of it."

"You seem to have a very short memory. You forget your relatives so easily."

"I was under the impression that they had forgotten me."

"Why?" she demanded in a pained tone.

"Oh well," he replied, a faint hint of shame in his voice, "I suppose I was no credit to the family, and I naturally thought they wouldn't want to see me again."

"Your mother died of grief because of you," said Gek Kim. He was silent and seemed to be struggling with sorrow and remorse. "You know, we all believed you to be innocent," she continued. "You didn't commit the crime, did you?"

For a moment he looked irresolute, as if he were searching for a suitable reply. Then he said in a growling tone, "Well, supposing I did, what then?

His guilt was now obvious, and she shuddered a little before she hesitantly answered, "Your own conscience knows best."

"I hope you are not going to begin a moral lecture," he said sarcastically. "I couldn't endure it, even from the lips of a hoary saint, to say nothing of a young girl."

She realised that his character had undergone radical changes, or perhaps more to the truth, his latent evil had now come to the surface. "How did you come here?"

"That's a long story. I did not come here at first. I wished to leave the country. But I fell in with a band of brave men like myself and I joined them. We came here only last year, after roaming in many places. When our leader died six months ago, I got my present position."

"You seem quite satisfied with your position."

"I certainly don't despise it."

"I suppose you never thought of reforming."

"Reforming?" he sneered. "Much good that will do me. I love my present life, thank you."

She saw that he was incorrigible. After a short pause she asked: "What do you intend to do with me?"

"I don't know. I must think first."

"You had better send me back as quickly as possible. You surely do not want our money."

"I will tell you my decision later."

He shouted for Crooked Mouth and gave him some instructions. Gek Kim was conducted to a smaller apartment near his; a creaking bed and a stool were soon installed there in her honour. They did not see each other again that day. The entrance to her room was closed by a kind of door, but it was not locked. She lay awake most of the night, pondering her predicament, the depravity of her cousin, what had happened to Sum Goh, and what anxieties her parents must be enduring on account of her disappearance. She recalled the prediction of the soothsayer, who had said with calm assurance, reinforced by his venerable white beard, that she was fated to suffer a serious calamity this year—and was not the prediction fulfilled? The explanation of the phenomenon was attributable to pure chance, of course, but it was strange, all the same. But, according to him, she would be restored to happiness, and she earnestly hoped that this prophecy would come true. She was half inclined to believe that, after all, the old man might really possess some mysterious source of knowledge, as desire ousted reason. At any rate, nothing really horrible could happen to her now, as her cousin, however sunk in infamy, could have no reason to do her any injury. She would undoubtedly go home tomorrow; having come to that comforting conclusion, she fell asleep and did not wake till late in the morning.

When she saw her cousin soon after, he wore a strange look of exultation, which did not harmonize well with his character, and much of his gloom had dissipated, as if by the touch of a magic wand. He spoke with as much gentleness and consideration as he could command and smoked his pipe with unaccountable gusto. Gek Kim was mildly surprised, and her mind tentatively made a partial reconstruction of her opinion of him in the light of such fresh knowledge. She waited for him to speak.

"This is a fine day, isn't it?" he remarked.

"I suppose so," she replied, her eyes casually sweeping the roof of the cave. She was tempted to inquire, no doubt humorously, how he managed to know the state of the day when all he knew of it was the pale light creeping through the apertures.

"I had a lovely dream last night," he said with a smile.

"Indeed! What might it have been?"

"Yes, a very lovely dream," he continued in a musing tone, hardly heeding her interruption. "I dreamed that you …"

"Oh, you dreamed about me! Thank you for the honour."

He roused from his reverie with a start and appeared slightly annoyed, but, determined to be gentle, he said smoothly, "Well, I have a very bad memory for dreams. I can never recall the details of a dream the moment I wake. I am afraid I can't remember last night's either. All I know is that it was a perfect dream, a happy dream. And it has made me come to a certain definite decision."

He looked at her curiously. She tried to be as cool as a cucumber.

"What decision?"

"I have come to the conclusion that I will not send you home," he said, almost chanting the words slowly.

"Why?" she looked puzzled.

"You will stay with me always."

"What for?" she asked with the innocence of a dove.

"I have thought over the problem, and I intend to marry you."

"You are not serious," she said with perfect calm.

"I was never more serious in my life. You know, Gek Kim, I have always liked you, from our earliest days, although I did not see much of you. Even during the last few years, whenever I thought of home, I thought of you." This was rather contradictory to the deduction that logically followed from his previous statement that he believed his relations had forgotten him, the deduction being that he naturally returned the compliment and never worried his head over them.

"I am glad you sometimes thought of me. But your suggestion that I should marry you is impossible."

"Why impossible?" he demanded with a slight, very slight, hint of impatience.

"You don't suppose that I shall be able to make a good robber," she said sarcastically.

"You don't have to do anything of the sort. You sit at home and we men do the work."

"And how do I obtain my food? Is it not the product of robbery?"

"You have ridiculously childish ideas," he said with a lofty air of condescension.

"In what way?"

"You will learn that after you have lived here for some time."

"And suppose I refuse to stay?"

"You are permitted to depart—if you can."

"So I am held prisoner in this place against my will."

"If you choose to put it that way, I suppose so. When a girl perversely refuses to listen to plain sense when gently offered, she will soon accept it, provided a little force is used. I regret to apply such constraint, but you will thank me for it later on."

"I hate you," she burst out with conviction. "I never imagined you could be so bad."

"Your hate will change to love later on. So I forgive you your words. If not for that consideration ..."

"You can kill me if you like. Were I to stay here ten thousand years, I should still hate you," she declared with an anger never experienced before in her life.

"We shall see."

She turned to leave and had reached the door before his strident voice arrested her graceful steps.

"Stop a moment. I wish to ask you something," he commanded sternly.

She paused, controlled her feelings of revulsion that the sight of him aroused, and stood with as much immobile dignity as was possible under the circumstances.

"You are not married, are you?"

She was so taken aback by the sudden question that she could not produce an immediate answer.

"Tell me the truth," he continued more sternly than ever. "You are not ashamed of your marriage, if you have entered into that state, I suppose."

Her pride was injured, and she retorted firmly: "I am not yet married, but I am engaged to be."

"The devil you are!" he exclaimed angrily, bringing his first down on the flimsy table with such force that it nearly collapsed. "Who is the man? Tell me everything about him."

Seeing no reason for concealment, and in fact feeling proud of her fiancé, especially after a swift comparison of him with this odious cousin of hers, she vouchsafed the information in calm, measured tones.

"You are only betrothed after all," he remarked, resuming a more normal state of composure. "It might have been worse."

"I do not understand in the least what you mean."

"You need not do so. Only that I might not love you so much if you were already married."

"Your love would not be regarded as a compliment by any woman."

"I am not so sure of that. Although we don't usually go in for kidnapping people, for it entails a lot of trouble, we have had a few girl captives, and I noticed they always liked me."

"You must be flattering yourself. You say that kidnapping is not your speciality. What is the reason that I was chosen for the honour of being a victim?"

"As I told you before, I did not give orders for the capture of any particular person. I don't think my lieutenant had it in mind to indulge in kidnapping when he set out for the town. I dare say he had his eye on your father's house, but, as for bringing you, he must have come to a sudden decision when he found that a convenient opportunity was offered," he explained. "It must have been fate that brought you. We are destined for each other," he added in a triumphant tone. He mused for a while, and then his face brightened with pleasure, approaching the diabolical. "As for the man to whom you are engaged, I am going to invite him here."

"You mean you are going to kidnap him?" she gasped, her heart beating painfully.

"It's more in the nature of an invitation," he declared, his loud laugh jarring on her nerves. "He shall renounce you. We won't injure him, since you would rather not, I dare say. But as compensation for the trouble of securing his presence, we will fix a modest ransom for his safe return. That will contribute to our wedding expenses," he concluded with a jocularity his victim failed to appreciate.

"You dare not do such an atrocious act!" she cried. She felt like swooning, as though a chasm were opening beneath her feet to plunge her into the midst of ferocious collection of hissing serpents, alert and intent, with fangs ready to torture her mercilessly.

"I dare not? You are yet ignorant of what I dare to do, if it pleases me," he sneered.

She retired with a superficial appearance of proud serenity, but once alone in her apartment, she gave way to the most poignant despair. Her fear for herself had vanished before the consuming fire of her concern for the welfare of Sum Goh. She deeply regretted that she had mentioned his name to the robber, and she could find no excuse for her folly. The question of paramount importance was how she could save him. She was determined to escape.

She carefully examined the room for any way out, but unfortunately, except through the door, there was none. It would not be easy to bore a hole through the solid rock, even if she possessed the necessary tools and could perform the task, both of which were impossible. She therefore had to rely upon the door, which was watched by the uncouth person whose name, Crooked Mouth, was derived from his principal distinguishing feature. He was sluggish by temperament, and, if he wasn't eating, his head was nodding on his bosom. Because he was not fit for active service, he had been chosen to dwell outside his master's room so that he might execute occasional orders of the more trifling sort. Now that she was here, he was supposed to keep a casual eye on her movements, but she was not really guarded because it was considered impossible that she could escape.

When night fell and all the robbers were apparently sound asleep, she tiptoed out of her room and gingerly passed by the sprawling form of Crooked Mouth, who was emitting the weirdest snores. She treaded softly along the passage and emerged into the cool night air, but on discovering herself in the middle of a gloomy, awe-inspiring forest, her dismay made her understand her cousin's confidence that she could never successfully escape from him. She was enclosed on all sides by trees, while hideous sounds rose and fell with nerve-racking persistence. However, she was determined to grope her way through the jungle, come what might, so with magnificent courage she began to step resolutely forward.

Unluckily, she had not gone many steps before she saw the silhouette of a man, standing erect between two trees. He unaccountably turned round and walked towards her. By the light of the half-moon she recognised the repellent features of her cousin; he had a pipe in his land and gazed at her with serene patience.

"Oh, it's you," he said, putting a fresh plug of tobacco in his pipe and lighting a match. "Found the cave too hot, I suppose. You have come for a breath of night air. So have I. You should have called Crooked Mouth to accompany you, though. I have given him orders to look after your comfort. I never dreamed you would have the courage to appear alone in the jungle. But it's getting late. We had better turn in."

He led her back into the cave and, before parting from her, added significantly, "We must take greater care of you in future and see that you do not go out alone again. You might meet up with dangerous wild beasts, perhaps."

CHAPTER 17

The Lure

When Sum Goh parted from Gek Kim at the foot of the shady tree, he went to the hut he had noticed, but the man there was embroiled in a tiff with his wife because he had used words of an unflattering description to refer to her family. Sum Goh could not make out exactly what the injurious terms that produced such an unhappy result were, for husband and wife started to explain to him the causes of the quarrel at the same time, and he was bewildered by the torrential flow of words. The upshot of the business was that he managed to put an end to the quarrel by using some amicable words whose lubricating qualities considerably reduced the friction of their marital discord. He then made known to the man what he wanted and purchased from him a couple of bottles of aerated water.

To his shock, however, on reaching the spot where he was sure he had left her standing, he discovered that Gek Kim was gone. She could not be trying to play hide and seek, as she had never done so before. He called her name many times, without hearing even an echo to comfort him. He scanned the surroundings, but, sadly enough, there were no traces of her at all. There was no clue on which to build a foundation. After wandering for some miserable hours hither and thither around the unhallowed region that contained the spring, he reluctantly abandoned his quest and went home to break the calamitous news.

The consternation of the two families concerned was great, and Mrs. Lee's grief was hardly less than that of Mrs. Low, and much more verbose. She severely reprimanded her son for his unpardonable carelessness in looking after Gek Kim and delivered a lengthy lecture in a memorable manner; she had never scolded him that way before. Lai Pek forgot about his commercial worries and was active in enlisting the help of the police, but, alas, the search was fruitless. Only Tua Sai was strangely free from worry about the fate of his daughter, as he possessed an optimistic belief that it was impossible she could be lost to him forever. He had never fully understood her ways, and doubtless she was now engaged in carrying out some mysterious whim and would return when she thought fit. But his wife did not share his optimism. On the second day of Gek Kim's absence, she journeyed to a temple built by a huge old tree, remarkable for its trunk, which, instead of being round, was in the form of an arc, and worshipped the god of the tree, vowing to offer him a goat in sacrifice two or three months after the safe return of her daughter, provided such a happy event materialised, of course.

As for Sum Goh, if ever there was a man who was on the point of qualifying himself for a cell in a lunatic asylum, he was that unfortunate being. Afflicted with the inability to eat or sleep, not knowing whether to stand or sit, talk or be silent, laugh or cry, he wandered restlessly through the house and out of it, his mind persistently beating to only one tune. *Where has she gone?* In his sorrow, he developed a passion for solitude and took to walking aimlessly round the lakes on the outskirts of the town.

On the evening of the third day after Gek Kim's disappearance, while sitting on a bench by the lake, utterly miserable, in fact contemplating the desperate idea of suicide, he was startled to hear a voice close to his ear. Turning around, he saw a man with a pleasant appearance; one of his hands, however, was in proud possession of six fingers. We know him very well as our old friend the pedlar; but Sum Goh was ignorant of his identity.

The man asked him his name, and, on receiving his answer, said with an air of mystery, "A young lady told me to give you a message. She said she was well and regretted that she had to keep herself away from home. You are to come immediately to her without telling anyone. She will explain everything to you when you see her. She is staying near the hot water spring. We are neighbours. In token of her continued affection for you, she asked me to hand you this."

The man placed in his palm a gold bracelet, which Sum Goh recognised as one of a pair that often adorned Gek Kim's wrists. His sorrow rushed away like a torrent, and joy—indescribable joy—flowed in to take its place at the same rate. He did not stop to question the genuineness of the message, or even to wonder what the peculiar cause was that prevented her from returning; all he knew was that he was going to see her again—explanations could very well be deferred.

"Let's go then!" he exclaimed, jumping into his car, which stood a few yards away.

The pedlar followed him in and smiled secretly to himself at the ease of his task. *What a simpleton this man is,* he thought, as he glanced at him out of the corner of his eye.

They soon came in view of the spring and alighted by the side of the road. The pedlar directed the way, and together they entered the forest, walking along at a nimble pace. Dusk was falling fast, and they had walked a tiresome distance when Sum Goh, awakening to the strangeness of his surroundings, asked where they were going.

"You will soon know," said the pedlar, and he displayed the identical pistol he had pointed at Gek Kim two days before.

At the same time, two men quietly appeared between the trees and began to trudge along in their company with stolid countenances, as if nothing usual were happening. Sum Goh realised with a shock the truth of Gek Kim's disappearance—she was in the hands of some unscrupulous scoundrels, and he was now also in their power. For a moment he was tempted to smash the face of the pedlar, but, thinking better of it, he controlled himself with an effort.

The robbers took out their flashlights and they all entered the cave. At the end of a short journey, which seemed to him of unearthly length, Sum Goh found himself in the presence of both the chief criminal and Gek Kim. The lovers cast an agonised look at one another, but they were unable to share any words at all before the brigand, who frowned ominously at any evidence of affection between them.

"So this is the young man to whom you are affianced," said the robber in not the pleasantest of tones, displaying his gross vulgarity in his triumph.

Sum Goh flushed at his coarse manner of speaking and took a step forward, with the full intention of inflicting corporal punishment on the robber, who richly merited such treatment.

"Stop!" warned the robber, producing a threatening pistol at the same time. "You are welcome to my apartment, but please keep a few feet away. Your arrival is most opportune," he continued, "we were just talking about you." Sum Goh glanced at Gek Kim, but she averted her eyes. "You may now know that this young lady is my cousin," he went on, just as severely as ever.

Sum Goh turned his face towards Gek Kim a second time, perfectly startled and hardly able to believe his ears, and she gave him a pathetic look, mingled with shame at the unenviable relationship. The chamber was lighted by a flickering oil lamp, and he could see beneath her superficial calmness evidence of the suffering she must have undergone the last few days.

“That is no fault of hers,” retorted Sum Goh, with something like a sneer on his lips.

“You may retire to your room,” said the robber to Gek Kim, and he called for Crooked Mouth to lead her away.

After her departure he said, assuming a portentous air, “And since you are here, you may also know that I loved her long before she ever saw you.”

Sum Goh started angrily but was restrained from committing any action by the play of the crook’s fingers around his pistol.

“The chief reason why I invited you here,” he continued, with a malicious inflection in his voice, “is to hear from your own lips that you renounce any claim to her.”

Sum Goh ground his teeth and muttered angrily, “Devil! I’ll first see you go back to hell before I do anything of the sort.”

“That’s your present opinion, I dare say. But it won’t last. I’m willing to restore you back to your family, if you do what I say. Otherwise ...”

“Otherwise, what?” sneered Sum Goh.

“You’ll meet with a fate you never dreamed of.”

“You can do your very worst,” challenged the indomitable Sum Goh. “No demon can ever make me perform the ignoble deed you dare to suggest.”

“We’ll see. Of course, it doesn’t matter much whether you explicitly dissolve your engagement with her or not. As far as

I'm concerned, it doesn't affect my intention that she should stay with me. I only want her to feel that she is not bound to you in any way."

"You think you can change her feelings by threatening me with force? So far as I can see, she must hate you like poison, and nothing will alter that. I'll never give her up."

"Your obstinacy will only bring an appropriate punishment on your head, which I would willingly spare you for her sake. I give you three days in which to think. I advise you to reconsider your decision, or you will pass out of this world altogether very soon."

Sum Goh smiled disdainfully and said in a musing tone, "I can't understand exactly how you came to be related to her family. Seems so outrageous."

The robber flushed darkly, but perhaps because he wanted to sleep or because he did not consider it worthwhile to inflict a trifling punishment on a man who was doomed to a major disaster, he simply ordered Crooked Mouth to lock Sum Goh up in a cell.

When Sum Goh was left alone, he paced up and down his cage in unwonted agitation. After calming down a bit, he was surprised to hear his name called, in most melodious tones. After some investigation, he found that the captivating voice came from a small hole in the wall, and he was agreeably astonished to discover that no less a person than Gek Kim was speaking to him.

"I heard you talking angrily as you passed my door and entered your room. What has that detestable cousin of mine been saying to you?"

"Nothing much, except that I was never to see you again."

"You won't give me up, will you?"

"I'll see him hanged first."

"How are the people at home?"

"Very distressed about your disappearance, of course."

"I mean, are they well?"

"Quite well, I think. Look here, Gek Kim, I am sorry I brought you to the cursed spring."

"As a matter of fact, it was I who suggested the visit. Don't worry. I am sure we'll be able to make our escape."

"Undoubtedly. And if I don't bring that robber to book—I hope you don't mind my calling your cousin a robber."

"You can call him anything you please. He is no credit to anybody. I hope you are comfortable," she added solicitously.

"Quite comfortable. Don't worry."

He looked perfunctorily around his bare cell, which was not provided with even a bed; the dirty rock floor was uneven and rough. Feeling a creeping sensation on his leg, he jerked it quickly, and a centipede crawled away.

"We'll talk about our plans for escape later on," said Gek Kim. "It's time to sleep."

Chapter 18

The Wrong Target

As Sin Beng Hu reclined in an elongated cane chair, his right arm under his head, he felt that life was very irksome, what with litigation, his business cares, and the need to rise every morning and go through a systematic ritual of shaving, bathing, and eating that never changed from day to day. He sighed and looked out of the window at a fine morning, too fine to waste in the shop. He longed for some stirring form of activity, some touch of the unusual, some fresh wind of adventure, even if attended by unpleasant results. However, as he realised only too vividly, romance was out of the question for a man enmeshed in a humdrum respectable life. He sighed again, much more deeply this time, and resolved not to go to work. But spending the day at home doing nothing would be even worse. Turning round, he noticed his gun resting in a cosy nook. He might as well go hunting; he had not pursued his favourite pastime for a month, and he would feel more zestful if he were to enter a forest he had never before visited.

With his chauffeur, who always followed him on his hunting expeditions, he arrived at the very jungle in which Sum Goh and Gek Kim were held captive, but the area where they had alighted was opposite the hot water spring. After walking a few steps, the men encountered a hut surrounded by a vegetable garden, which showed signs of painstaking industry and care. The cultivator himself was working among the furrows, but on seeing two men approach, he straightened his back, wiped his brow with his sleeve, and, though he betrayed some surprise on finding that one of them carried a formidable gun, politely asked them to make themselves at home in his humble abode. The invitation was not declined, and Beng Hu was soon trying to get information about the nature of the forest from their host.

"I have never seen any big beasts here," said the gardener. "There may be a few wild boars, though. Some time ago I saw one at a distance."

"I hope I meet that particular animal. I'll give it to you."

"You are very good, sir. However," he added hesitatingly, "I would rather you don't enter the forest."

"Why?" asked Beng Hu, his curiosity piqued.

"To tell you the truth, I suspect that it is the haunt of evil characters—robbers, probably."

"Why do you think so?"

"I have seen some suspicious persons within its boundaries many times. I don't see what they do for a living. I am sure they are here for no good purpose."

"Did they ever threaten to harm you?"

"I can't say that ever happened. But then they could hope to get nothing out of me. As a matter of fact, I believe they are among my customers. Of course, I have so far kept my suspicions to myself. For one thing, they are only suspicions. Besides," he added sadly, "I am only a poor man, dwelling here alone and entirely dependent upon this plot of ground for my living. If I were to poke my nose into their affairs or incur their displeasure in any way, they might think nothing of killing me outright, if they are really evil people. I hope you would not tell others what I tell you."

"Don't be afraid. I won't let you come to any harm."

The gardener smiled in relief, a frank, honest smile. "I only told you what I thought because I didn't wish you to fall into any danger."

"I know. After your kind warning I'll keep a sharp lookout and avoid tumbling into any snare."

They left the industrious vegetable gardener to resume his interrupted labour and proceeded briskly into the forest, which to Beng Hu seemed quite an adventurous place now. Covered with a luxuriant growth of tall grass and gigantic trees, it looked quite sinister, although intriguing. Owing to the incalculable vagaries of luck, before he had gone far, a boar of a goodly size crossed his vision for an instant when it emerged into an open space; then, before he could so much as point his gun in the proper direction, it disappeared into the tall grass. He began to stalk it with patient alertness, its movements revealed by the agitation of the wild growth it plunged through. For about five minutes he lost all track of his quarry, and he thought it had escaped him for good. Wanting to hazard a shot if it should reappear, his gun all ready for slaughter, he observed with the lustful joy of the hunter a faint stirring among the grass, suggesting the passage of the animal. Beng Hu pulled the trigger and fired.

A muffled scream, which bore not the faintest resemblance to the sound emitted by any wild boar that had the misfortune to cross his path, reached his ears. With his attendant following close behind him, he rushed towards the spot that hid the target of his bullet. What a sight greeted him—a veritable tribute to his skill in hunting! A man in a black cotton suit, with a small but capable body and an unprepossessing face, sat on the ground nursing a broken leg. A big, raw wound, splashed with arterial red blood, gaped midway between the knee and ankle of his left limb. The man scowled in a most unattractive manner, dampening Beng Hu's pity, though his conscience was struck with lively horror at his own ill-timed deed; he cursed himself under his breath. It was a matter of undeserved good fortune that he would not have to answer for the crime of homicide, with the death of a human being weighing heavily on his soul.

Calling into service his two clean white handkerchiefs and one belonging to his driver, he bandaged the man's wound as well as he could. Because the bone had sustained a fracture, the man's mobility was seriously impaired, and Beng Hu suggested he be conveyed to a hospital, but the unfortunate victim's response was not enthusiastic; instead he asked them in a surly voice to leave him alone. Astonished by such unaccountable behaviour, Beng Hu was ready to argue with him; then his eye fell on a scrap of paper lying two feet away in the grass. There was no particular reason why he should take any interest in a piece of paper without any distinguishing characteristic lying on the ground; still he stepped forward, picked it up, and glanced over the scribbled contents.

What he saw was a message, addressed to Lee Lai Pek, containing no signature of any sort. It stated that the latter could have his son back on payment of twenty thousand dollars, which was to be placed that very night at ten o'clock in a specified spot outside Lanta, or else he would never see him again. He was requested not to indulge in any tricks and not to inform the police or anyone else about the affair. Otherwise he would regret it for the rest of his life.

To say that Beng Hu was surprised at the missive is to give but a faint idea of his response—he stood perfectly dumb and confounded; his eyes could not blink or his legs stir. He knew—the whole town knew—that Lee Lai Pek's son, as well as his future daughter-in-law, had disappeared in some mysterious fashion; but Beng Hu had not given any thought to the problem, partly because he never imagined that any particular significance was attached to these events. Now, however, he held a clue to the mystery, and he recalled that they had both vanished near that very forest. The young man's car had been found the previous morning, abandoned a short distance from the spring near the roadside. The vegetable gardener's warning that there might be robbers dwelling thereabouts came into his mind. His perusal of the letter and his thoughts took only a minute. Then he heard the voice of his chauffeur saying impatiently to the wounded man, "You are not going to sit here till the wound is healed, I suppose. Where is your house? We'll take you there."

His mind abruptly returned to earth. The wounded man, who till then had been sullenly contemplating his injuries, now turned round and perceived the scrap of paper that Beng Hu had unconsciously let fall near him, face downwards. With a perceptible start, he quickly stretched out his hand, grabbed it, and was about to place it in his pocket, when Beng Hu said, "Wait a moment. The paper is yours, I presume."

"Certainly!" blurted out the man, startled. "It must have dropped out of my pocket when I fell down from your cursed shot."

"What does it contain?"

"What business is it of yours?" retorted the man. "Is it not enough that you have shot me—I could have you arrested for the crime—but you must also ask what I carry with me? If you want to know, it contains a list of things I intend to buy in town."

"With money obtained from the ransom of a man?"

The unlucky wretch looked confused and trembled so violently that there was danger of further injuries, not only to his wounded limb, but to his entire body.

"Where do you live?" asked Beng Hu sternly.

"Deep inside this forest."

"Are you a member of a gang of robbers?"

"Yes. What are you going to do with me?"

"We'll take you to the nearest hut first. We can talk more comfortably there."

Beng Hu and his curious driver then helped the man to move along slowly until they reached the house of the vegetable gardener, who was surprised at the peculiar manner of their return. He recognised the wounded man, as he had seen him a few times before, and greeted him politely. He was disappointed to receive no corresponding answer. When they were safely inside the hut, the driver took the gardener aside and whispered that the man was a brigand; after registering an appropriate amount of shock, the gardener replied that he was not really astonished, because the man was one of the evil characters he had sometimes encountered. He was rather dismayed to have a robber in his house, even though it boasted no tempting articles; nevertheless, he kept his silence.

Beng Hu was questioning the robber with punctilious minuteness. "Are both the girl and the young man still safe?"

"Yes. They have not been subjected to any ill treatment.

"Why is it that only the man is held to ransom, although he disappeared later than the girl?"

"I can't tell you, as that depends upon our chief."

"How does one reach the cave in which you people dwell?"

The robber described in detail the route to the required destination. All his courage, if he ever possessed any, together with his sullenness, had disappeared, and he was evidently giving away all the necessary information. He was not one of those daredevil brigands who gloried in their achievements—he was only a tool of others.

"Is the cave guarded?" asked Beng Hu.

What did it matter to him whether it was or wasn't? "Never. It is supposed to be safe from intrusion, as no one would dream of venturing into it. Besides, since the capture of the two young people, our chief has been more indulgent towards us, and today he has allowed most of the men to leave the forest to go and enjoy themselves in various places. Those who stay in the cave usually spend their afternoons sleeping."

Why should Beng Hu feel great joy on hearing all this? He did, and if it had not been inconsistent for someone of his dignity, he would have executed a somersault in the air. His chauffeur was perplexed to discover that his employer had not looked so happy in a long time. The explanation lay in the fact that Beng Hu was experiencing the pleasant sensation of being among the mysteries of high and thrilling adventure. He would take a peek at a robbers' den, a strange spot that exuded sinister attraction.

And then he thought of the son and future daughter-in-law of Lee Lai Pek, his rival. He felt great sympathy for them, and he determined he must do something on their behalf. True, he was on bad terms with Lee Lai Pek. Still, such a minor affair must be drowned in the sea of oblivion when a great calamity like this was considered. Besides, his quarrel with the father did not permit him to hate the son, and still less the girl. He must rescue them himself.

Full of this noble resolution, he shouldered his gun, drew himself erect, and assumed such a formidable expression that the modest vegetable gardener was daunted. He asked, disconcerted, "Where are you going, sir?"

"To the robbers' cave."

"What?" exclaimed the man with horrified incredulity, forgetting his manners, for the time being fully persuaded that the respectable stranger must have taken leave of his senses.

"I am quite sane," laughed Beng Hu as he noted the man's look. Laughter was not one of his prominent characteristics, and he must have been in rare spirits to do so at that moment.

The gardener did not know where to look in his utter confusion over this response, but Beng Hu soon enlightened him concerning his purpose in wishing to pay a visit to such an ominous spot by providing a brief account of what he knew about the kidnapping. The peasant lifted both his hands in an attitude of prayer, calling upon Heaven to punish the outrageous robbers, and offered to accompany Beng Hu on his noble venture, which to his disappointment was declined with thanks.

"Too many people might jeopardise our task," said Beng Hu. "You stay here and take care of this wounded robber till we return. You'll know where we are and will be able to help if anything should happen to us."

Chapter 19
Escape

Beng Hu and his attendant—who relished the coming experience hardly less than his master, for he had been an adventurer in his earlier days and half a dozen times had indulged in various escapades that had nearly brought to an untimely close his existence in the present world—left the hut on speedy feet. They traced the route described by the wounded robber without much difficulty; the chauffeur possessed such a keen and reliable sense of direction that he seemed to be an animated compass. They met with no dangerous animals on their journey, and indeed Beng Hu's enthusiasm for wild boars was so much abated that it was unlikely he would have risked a shot, even if the most tempting specimen had crossed his path.

They travelled efficiently and arrived in the region of the caves without needing to rest. From that point, they proceeded more slowly and warily, and they soon stood before the mouth of the cave they sought. With commendable courage, they immediately scouted its inhospitable length, hugging the more shadowy portions as much as possible. Beng Hu had his gun ready in case of emergency, and his attendant clutched a nasty dagger. Within a quarter of an hour, they were observing the prostrate form of Crooked Mouth, blissfully slumbering. The driver bent down, closed his ill-constructed mouth with one palm, and gently shook him. Soon Crooked Mouth opened his languid eyes. Seeing a dagger close to his throat and a threatening face above him, he began to think that he was having a particularly ugly dream, when disturbing, whispering sounds floated above him.

When the driver saw that Crooked Mouth was fully awake—the terror in his eyes would have satisfied the most sadistic temperament——he whispered in a tone that meant business, "We want to find the man and the girl who were kidnapped. Where are they?"

He withdrew his hand, and Crooked Mouth scrambled to his feet. With his still unquenched thirst for sleep, the consuming fear that manifested itself in uncouth trembling, prodigiously ridiculous to behold, and his natural inability to speak in other than a hoarse mutter, it was extremely difficult to understand what he was saying. So Beng Hu cut him short by demanding that he bring them to where the persons he sought were confined. Crooked Mouth produced a bunch of keys from a small pocket in his broad leather belt and unlocked a door.

As the door was slowly pulled open by the driver, a touching sight greeted Beng Hu's sympathetic eyes. Gek Kim, seated on her crazy-looking stool, was sobbing uncontrollably, releasing the unbearable anguish in her heart, for she had almost given up hope of ever escaping from that detested hole; she feared the worst for Sum Goh, whom, she now knew, her cousin had threatened to kill the next day. She looked up, fully expecting to see her inquisitor, prepared to assume a proud, uncompromising attitude, when she was amazed to see instead the kindly face of Beng Hu. She was about to speak when he stepped forward, told her to maintain strict silence, and led her out of the room. She obeyed with remarkable docility.

Crooked Mouth next opened the door of the cell in which Sum Goh was imprisoned. That gentleman, his clothing soiled and dishevelled, was waiting with an angry face, his eyes fixed on the roof, which, if it had any feelings at all, would have split asunder; indeed it had a tolerably long, though shallow, fissure. He was quite oblivious to the presence of his rescuers and came to life only when Gek Kim touched him on the arm. He looked from her to Beng Hu with an uncomprehending stare, but with a few well-chosen words she apprised him of the situation, and with alacrity he moved towards the door. Crooked Mouth, who had entered the cell, was about to follow him. Beng Hu whispered some words into the ear of his attendant, who forthwith silenced the inglorious brigand with a gag. Procuring a rope, which happened to be hanging just outside the door, in use as a clothesline, he next dexterously tied up the robber's arms and legs as he lay on the floor.

"You will now be able to resume your interrupted sleep," murmured the driver, surveying his handiwork with genuine satisfaction. He had never felt so pleased with any job. Crooked Mouth looked most grotesque in his undignified position. "Don't be afraid," continued the driver, "when you awake, doubtless your comrades will release you."

They all passed out of the room, save the outraged robber, and Beng Hu locked the door. In a short time they stood beside the entrance to the cave.

"All danger is not yet past," said Beng Hu. "We are not safe until we reach the town."

They set off at a trot and continued in absolute silence till they reached the hut of the vegetable gardener, by which time night had fallen. The gardener himself stood at his unostentatious door and welcomed them effusively, truly glad to see them. After some time, however, he assumed a rueful expression, which did not escape Beng Hu's notice. "Did anything happen during our absence?" asked Beng Hu with concern.

"That wounded robber you left with me escaped about an hour ago."

"Escaped! How did he manage that?"

"I was chopping firewood behind the house, and I must confess I left him alone for quite a long time. I never imagined he could walk. Besides, I thought he would be quite willing to go along with you on your return."

"He was evidently not as helpless as we fancied. He must have been able to move, I dare say with difficulty. Never mind. His flight is of no special importance."

"I wonder where he could have gone."

"He must be still in the forest, crawling back to their den. Poor fellow! He is certain to find dragging himself along unusually painful. I wouldn't care to be in his place."

Sum Goh, who since their arrival in the hut, had been talking aside to Gek Kim, now turned towards Beng Hu diffidently and said, "How can we express our thanks to you, Mr. Sin, for our deliverance?"

"No need for any," said Beng Hu, lighting a cigarette. "Only too pleased to help you."

Sum Goh was not exactly ignorant of the relationship between Beng Hu and his father, who several times had made unflattering allusions to his rival in the presence of his family, and, though he had taken no part at all in the commercial war, he still felt it was doubly magnanimous of Beng Hu to come to their rescue. Sum Goh had hardly ever come in contact with him before, and had never appreciated him, but now he was overwhelmed with gratitude.

"How did you two get yourselves kidnapped?" asked Beng Hu after a pause, turning himself round in the chair to look at them with great curiosity.

Gek Kim told her story first, in as few words as possible, and Sum Goh followed suit. The vegetable gardener listened open-mouthed, from time to time scratching his head in wonder. During the course of Gek Kim's recital, he gasped, "Monstrous!" and while Sum Goh was giving his narrative, "Barbarous!" Other than these two expressive comments, he had nothing more to say.

"Sounds rather adventurous," said Beng Hu, after they had both finished.

"I must confess I felt nothing but the greatest abhorrence for our misfortune. I did not feel a single thrill. Did you like our adventure, Gek Kim?"

"Not in the least!" exclaimed Gek Kim, in a tone palpably tinged with disgust. "You remember I told you that I did not love a monotonous life, but this kind of stimulation is not to my taste."

Beng Hu emitted a quiet, amused laugh. "It is clear that neither of you would be willing to enter into a hazardous enterprise for its own sake. Doubtless you find your experience disconcerting now, but you will look back on it with interest later."

"I hope so," said Sum Goh glumly. "I don't think I'll ever forget it, in any case. Those brigands …"

The vegetable gardener was rather alarmed by the unappealing prospect of having to endure the presence of a whole gang of robbers, who might in their egregious villainy deliver upon him a dire revenge, but he attempted to look as brave as possible. When Beng Hu said to him, "You might as well come with us. You can return here if you like when the forest is cleared of the brigands, and that won't be long," he was vastly relieved and made no effort to conceal his approval of the plan.

They swiftly drove back to Lanta. The night wind blew chill against their faces and sang in a discordant tune, while eerie noises, some of which sounded like the laughter of demons, erupted from the inhospitable land on either side of the road, which was rough and narrow. But high up, the moon, now in its third quarter, looked down upon them with benign serenity. They were all silent and, judging from their expressions, obviously wrapped in thought. Beng Hu, glad that he had been able to combine adventure with altruistic service, sat with impressive gravity. The driver, who was not so free to indulge in contemplation as the others if he were to avoid imperilling their lives, looked straight ahead. However, the thought crossed his mind that he would become the centre of interest among his cronies when he related his story in a coffee shop, and this made him silently bless the lucky day. The vegetable gardener fervently hoped that the robbers would not go to his hut and demolish it or ruthlessly trample over his crops. Sum Goh longed for revenge against the man who tried to take his most valuable treasure away from him and regretted that he had been so powerless against him in the den. Gek Kim was sunk in the events of the last few days, and, glancing at the moon, she reflected, with a touch of poetic fancy, how like the moon is life—now a sparkling orb of bliss, then a dark mass of misery, but for the most part a combination of happiness and pain, blended in varying proportions.

At last they reached the town. After depositing Sum Goh and Gek Kim at their respective doorsteps, politely declining their invitations to alight, as he did not want to receive the embarrassing thanks of their parents, Beng Hu drove home. Mrs. Sin, who had begun to fear that her husband was another victim, vanishing suddenly and irrevocably, was overjoyed to find him returned safe and sound.

On information provided by Beng Hu, a squad of policemen was sent early the next morning to arrest the brigands, but when they reached the cave they found it deserted. The criminals must have come to the conclusion that it wasn't safe to dwell in their abode any further and fled to seek a more favourable refuge.

However, the chief of the band, the disreputable cousin of the spotless Gek Kim, was captured nearly a year later in another part of the country and was consigned to his proper place in prison.

Chapter 20

Reconciliation

Lai Pek had been extremely concerned at the loss of Gek Kim, but the subsequent disappearance of his son put the finishing touch to his grief. He racked his brain for a solution to the problem, but though that admirable organ functioned well enough in connection with commerce, it was quite helpless when confronted with such untoward occurrences, out of the course of normal life. He even went so far as to lose all interest in business; he became absent-minded and behaved more or less like an automaton. His despair was mercifully shortened, without doubt as a reward for some virtuous deed in a previous life, when Sum Goh presented himself at home in an unseemly condition. Lai Pek was bereft of speech for fully five minutes when he learned that Sin Beng Hu was the cause of his son's happy return.

On the morning after the fortuitous rescue of Sum Goh and Gek Kim, Lai Pek was alone with his wife in undisturbed conversation.

"How ironic fate is!" remarked Lai Pek with a grave expression. "To think that our son should owe his safety to our enemy!"

"I don't know why you ever conceived a dislike for Mr. Sin Beng Hu," said Mrs. Lee, a shadow of regret flitting over her face. "He always seemed to me a very inoffensive person."

"We won't go into that question now," responded Lai Pek hastily. "If I was not favourably disposed towards him, it was for business reasons, which could not be expected to appeal to you. However, if I don't go and thank him for his noble deed, it would be churlish. If I do go, how can I preserve my face in front of him? I would have to admit I was responsible for the disgraceful war against him."

"If you don't go," Mrs. Lee stated firmly, "you will lose all your face in the town. Every man will condemn you."

"Here is a pretty situation," sighed Lai Pek. "I can't understand why such a thing should happen to me."

"Ask yourself another question," replied Mrs. Lee in an encouraging tone. "Why should you be so favoured by the gods as to have your son back?"

"I suppose my visit is inevitable," concluded Lai Pek resignedly.

Mrs. Lee nodded her approval.

An hour afterwards, Lai Pek, feeling most uncomfortable, stood before the residence of Sin Beng Hu. Thrice he turned to leave, with his mission unaccomplished, but at last summoning up his resolution, he entered the porch. An interesting scene met his eyes; a group of boys, including the son and heir of the house, were intently watching the contents of a large clear glass bowl. Two fighting fishes, displaying beautiful dark green scales, were viciously biting each other with martial enthusiasm and exemplary courage. They swam round and round in watchful proximity, their elegant tails spread out like fans and their gills distended haughtily, seeking a good opportunity for attack. They rapidly exchanged a succession of stinging bites, with the result that scales flew and fins were torn off. Once, their mouths became locked in a mutual embrace, and it was some time before they separated. They maintained their stubborn bravery a good while before one suddenly lost heart and fled before the other; its tail closed, its gleaming colours vanquished. The boy who owned the defeated fish looked crestfallen and had to forfeit it to him who was in proud possession of the victor.

Lai Pek watched the contest to its conclusion before he inquired of Beng Hu's son whether his father was at home.

"Yes, he is," said the boy happily, for it was he who had just won the fish.

"Will you please tell him that I wish to see him?"

The boy ceased feeding his row of fishes with mosquito larvae and ran into the house. After a few minutes Beng Hu himself emerged and gravely invited Lai Pek in.

"Take a seat," said Beng Hu with ceremonious courtesy. "Put yourself at ease."

Lai Pek was so much at ease that he felt a tingling sensation in his face, a sensation very rare for him, at any rate to such a degree.

"I wish, Mr. Sin," began Lai Pek after some uncomfortable hesitation, "to express my worthless thanks for your matchless kindness in delivering my son."

"Truly, Mr. Lee, you embarrass me," was the equally polite rejoinder. "Any little help that I could render is not worth mentioning."

"You are too modest. My son might not be alive but for you."

"Really, you exaggerate his danger," murmured Beng Hu.

"Not at all," staunchly insisted Lai Pek. "I know the full story. And I also know," he smiled, "that you saved me twenty thousand dollars."

"How's that?" asked Beng Hu innocently.

"I heard, through the stories your driver narrated to many people, that the brigands wanted that amount as ransom."

"Oh! I am sure you would not have given it without a fight."

"All men are not as brave as you are, Mr. Sin."

"Your politeness is really excessive."

Having disposed of this topic, Lai Pek proceeded to one even more delicate. He looked out of the window for a moment, was seized with a fit of coughing, and said, "I also have to apologize for the unfortunate nature of our last meeting. I hope you will kindly forget what I said."

"The fault was wholly mine. I should not have accused your company of such an act."

"Not at all. You had the right to suspect us of it. I am not quite sure even now," admitted Lai Pek, gazing out of the window a second time, "as to how those atrocious cakes came into the market. Probably, without my knowledge, some indefensible doings were carried on in our shop."

Beng Hu was silent, as he did not know exactly what to say.

"I am sorry we ever came in competition with one another," said Lai Pek after a pause. "What do you say if we sell our confectionery to you?"

Beng Hu registered immense surprise. "How could you wish to do so?" he asked.

"I never really cared for the enterprise," was the reply. "If you would be so kind as to take it off my hands, I should be grateful for it."

To Lai Pek, trade was the sauce of life, making his days interesting. But his struggle with cakes had been none too appealing, and he was in truth little attracted by the confectionery.

"Have all your partners agreed to its sale?"

"No. In fact I haven't told them about my intention yet."

"They may refuse to part with it."

"That's a possibility. But I don't think it's probable. I'll try to persuade them. In any case, even if they refuse my suggestion, I am definitely through with it. I'll withdraw my capital, and, not having enough of their own to carry on, they will have to close it down."

"I hope you are not putting yourself to inconvenience for my sake," said Beng Hu uneasily.

"None whatsoever. I am really sick of the venture."

"I think I was wrong to come butting in on your long-established business," admitted Beng Hu, after pressing on his guest a steaming cup of tea. "I must confess, though, I did not think that it would do you any harm. If you don't mind, we'll come to a suitable agreement between ourselves as to the kinds of goods we'll sell. If you wish to deal in any particular variety, I'll refrain from that."

"You are remarkably generous," responded Lai Pek with deep appreciation.

"And if your partners, on whose province I may have encroached, would like this kind of proposal, I'll do the same for them."

"They'll be enthusiastic supporters of it."

"As for the lawsuit, which my misdirected mind first started ..."

"You were justified ..."

"We'll call it off," affirmed Beng Hu, without breaking the flow of his words.

"This day marks an epoch in my humble life," said Lai Pek with feeling. "Of course, I shall pay all the legal expenses you incurred, as it would only be just."

"No need for any such magnanimity on your part."

"I must, I must!" insisted Lai Pek. "I could do no less after causing you so much trouble."

"The trouble was of my own seeking. To oblige me, I hope you wouldn't press on me a cent."

Lai Pek reluctantly gave up the polite struggle.

An amiable solution having been reached and all discordant issues satisfactorily settled, both were immensely relieved and began to chat freely on a variety of light topics. When Lai Pek was on the point of departure, visitors were announced. In stepped Heow Tu, Tow Lia, and several others. The new guests were surprised at Lai Pek's presence, though they concealed it perfectly. There then succeeded a series of bows and pleasant greetings, very eloquent in the bracing atmosphere of friendliness. Tow Lia seemed to be possessed of some important message but experienced great difficulty in delivering it before Lai Pek, at whom he gazed uneasily, coughing solemnly. Lai Pek however lightened his anxiety by remarking, "Doubtless all you gentlemen know what a great service Mr. Sin rendered me yesterday. I have just been expressing to him my most inadequate thanks."

The new guests all smiled with relief.

"One informs ten; ten inform a hundred," said Tow Lia pleasantly. "The whole town has heard of his bravery."

"His achievement has never been paralleled in Lanta," added the portly Heow Tu.

"Marvellous indeed," interposed a guest with a gold tooth.

"I was struck dumb with incredulity when I heard of it," said a gentleman with a white beard.

"Its glory will forever dwell in our remembrance," chimed in another, who possessed a mole on his right cheek.

"It deserves to be made the subject of a ballad," fitly concluded the last of the visitors, who, sadly enough, possessed no distinguishing characteristic in his appearance.

Beng Hu blushed under the collective weight of the eulogies, which were pronounced with a portentous degree of gravity.

"Such words about one of my inferior achievements …"

"We are extremely proud of you," asserted all the guests, including Lai Pek, who endeavoured to look as if he had loved Beng Hu like a brother from childhood and nothing untoward had ever marred their mutual esteem.

"We have come here today," began Tow Lia, with an air befitting such a momentous occasion, "not out of idle curiosity with regard to your remarkable exploit. We wish, first, to express our deep appreciation for your character and, secondly, to offer you a concrete proposition. You know, in a few days' time, the annual election of office bearers in our club is due to take place. We shall feel extremely honoured if you would consent to become its chairman."

Like electric lamps at the touch of a common switch, all his fellow visitors simultaneously assumed blissful expressions.

"This is very sudden," said Beng Hu modestly. "A complete surprise to me."

"Not a disagreeable one, I hope," responded Heow Tu, driving an imaginary fly from his shoes with his walking stick.

"It would be presumptuous of me to aspire to such an honour," replied Beng Hu, consistent in his decorous behaviour. "I am one of the newest members of the club."

"Merit counts more with us than length of connection," stated Heow Tu agreeably. "Your election will meet with unanimous approval."

"I am grateful to all of you for the kindness shown me," said Beng Hu, not deficient in the quality of being agreeable. "I'll think over your proposal."

"We absolutely insist upon your acceptance," pressed Tow Lia, "unless you have any special objections against the post."

"No, I can have no objections."

"Then," interjected Tow Lia triumphantly, "you must accede to our offer."

"I suppose I must," conceded Beng Hu, giving up the struggle.

“Excellent!” exclaimed Tow Lia and Heow Tu together.

“We have wasted too much of your valuable time already,” said Heow Tu rising.

Beng Hu saw them to the door, and Lai Pek took his departure along with them. On the way home, Heow Tu and the others refrained from questioning him about his visit to Beng Hu, nor did he vouchsafe any information.

That afternoon Lai Pek called a meeting of his partners and announced his proposal to transfer the confectionery to Beng Hu. After recovering from their momentary surprise, they all roundly condemned the suggestion, saying it would be the height of insanity to abandon such a prosperous concern. Hwey Pin was decidedly furious and expressed his disapproval in no uncertain words.

“Business is business,” he asserted with ungraceful force, “and sentiment is sentiment. We are not ignorant of your debt to him, but that can be repaid in better fashion than by jeopardizing our interests, even if you don’t care for yours.”

“I *am* talking business,” responded Lai Pek coldly. “I don’t think it would be of much benefit to us to carry the company further. We have already incurred a great deal of trouble and expense in connection with our lawsuit, and there is every possibility of our losing the case. If so, our business will be ruined and our fair name tarnished.”

“We can never lose the suit,” declared Hwey Pin vehemently.

“How do you know that?” demanded Lai Pek with dignity. “Even our lawyer, whom I interviewed a week ago, was by no means optimistic. Besides, we began this company partly in the hope of brightening our individual prospects. I cannot say that we have succeeded to any great extent. But now we can recover most of our former prosperity. Sin Beng Hu has suggested that we should not encroach on one another's markets."

"What!" exclaimed a morose-looking individual.

Lai Pek explained Beng Hu's proposal. Half the partners were immediately in favour of transferring their concern in the confectionary venture.

"If you people don't want to sell the company," stated Lai Pek, "you can carry on yourselves. I am withdrawing my capital."

All the partners were convinced without any further hesitation, except Hwey Pin, who after a time also had to yield, although with very bad grace, when he found himself pressed by irrefutable arguments on all sides. His association with Lai Pek completely ceased from that time onwards, in terms of business and otherwise.

Chapter 21

The Wedding

After a blissful period, during which no further trouble arose to cast a malignant shadow or threaten to separate them from each other, the propitious day arrived for the marriage of Sum Goh and Gek Kim. The date was specially chosen by the old soothsayer of Toliu based on an accurate reading of their horoscopes; even the hour when the ceremony should take place was established. With such an auspicious beginning, their marriage could not help but turn out to be a glorious success.

All the preparations were complete, down to the minutest details. Invitations had been duly dispatched to all the relatives and friends of both families, and in response a magnificent stream of presents arrived—perfume, handkerchiefs, cloth, vases, and jewellery—to attest to the everlasting esteem and sincere goodwill of the donors.

Gaiety and ceremonies were not confined to the wedding day—they reigned both before and after. Both houses were hung with red silk bunting, and brocaded curtains waved over the doorways. Every passerby knew from their external appearances that a marriage was due to take place inside them. In front of each house were placed two large round cloth lanterns with painted red characters. The eve of the nuptials was of special importance in the bride's household, as on the morrow she would move to a new abode.

While the bride was still with them, a feast was given by Low Tua Sai, and his two brothers, the fat and the tall, attended. The latter felt rather scandalised that his niece was already well acquainted with the bridegroom. He declared that his daughters would certainly not be allowed to behave thus, but as no one paid any heed to his opinions, he wisely put them aside and contented himself with his share of the excellent viands. He looked rather morose, though; when rallied by the fat brother, who was in the height of good humour and went about exchanging greetings with everybody, he just dumbly shook his head and murmured some incoherent words.

The residence of Lai Pek had never before presented such a scene of bustling activity and decorative splendour. Everyone rose very early, including the relatives and the most intimate friends of the family, who had arrived two or three days before.

"This promises to be a fine day," said Lai Pek.

"I hope so," replied his spouse, "otherwise half our pleasure will be gone. Do you remember our wedding? Such ..."

"A great downpour of rain," interposed Lai Pek. "Quite unexpected. What a spoiler a shower can be!"

He then fell into a wistful train of thought and returned to the moment with a start when Mrs. Lee asked, "Have you a list of the guests who sent us gifts?"

"Yes, a very long one," replied Lai Pek with genuine satisfaction. "I never knew we were so popular before," he added with becoming modesty.

"I trust you have not omitted to send any of them a card of thanks," commented Mrs. Lee.

Sum Goh was in a state of nervous anxiety regarding the forthcoming ceremonies. However, he duly proceeded to bring the bride home, and they were officially introduced at the tea ceremonies, each to the members of the other's family.

As they sat in the bridal chamber in his father's house, Sum Goh looked at Gek Kim with a proud, happy expression, more eloquent than any phrases he could articulate. They were properly united in the bonds of matrimony, and nothing could separate them now. Although she did not glow with exultation—permissible in a man but unbecoming to a newly married bride, as any of her seniors could have told her—she was no less happy in reality. For a time they were silent, each feeling the awkwardness of the situation. Soon Sum Goh cleared his throat and observed, "What a tiring day! You are not unduly fatigued, I hope."

"No! Did I seem nervous?"

"All brides are supposed to be shy," he answered lightly. "But you didn't seem timid at all. You were your usual captivating self."

"Don't talk nonsense. In reality, I felt embarrassed."

From below floated a hubbub of voices, mingled with loud laughter; the women guests were enjoying the bountiful banquet prepared for their exclusive benefit. Some of them were very happy indeed, because they had just found prospective husbands for their daughters or wives for their sons among the friends of the bridegroom and bride. Several elderly ladies who clung to existence principally for the purpose of promoting marriages were busy pointing out desirable bachelors to inquisitive mothers. It was all extremely exhilarating.

"What are you thinking about?" asked Sum Goh, noting a sad, dreamy look in Gek Kim's eyes.

"Oh, nothing! I was just struck by a memory of the brigands' cave."

"A very unpleasant subject," frowned Sum Goh. "I have completely forgotten about that."

"That's admirable," said Gek Kim in sweet agreement. "It's what I have tried to do, though sometimes I can't help thinking about it."

"My old soothsayer was right in his prediction, at least in part. You met with serious trouble, and you were safely delivered from it. The other part—I can't say whether you have attained your desire or not, as I don't know what it is."

"You know it very well," laughed Gek Kim. "He was completely right by chance."

"Come, come," said Sum Goh seriously. "He must be more than a charlatan after this last demonstration of his skill."

Gek Kim evaded a definite answer. "Anyway, whatever he might be, I like him for your sake."

"I'm sorry," said Sum Goh gloomily. "I didn't appear very heroic in that unfortunate business. I could not destroy the brigands by force or come up with a successful plan for our escape."

"You are always yourself," said Gek Kim consolingly, "and that is much more important to me than occasional stunts."

Evening soon came, and the clock struck eight, its tones melodious to the numerous people who came to attend the feast given by Lai Pek. Spreading through several spacious rooms—glorious with new paint, ablaze with fanciful lanterns bearing gorgeous designs descriptive of historical and legendary scenes, and rendered enchanting by flowers of diverse hues—were carefully laid tables, waiting to receive the dishes supplied by a crew of expert cooks who were specially engaged for the occasion.

As the guests entered, singly or in small groups, Lai Pek received them; everyone expressed congratulations on his marvellous good fortune in having a wedded son, and the host replied appropriately. The majority consisted of Lai Pek's personal acquaintances from his own generation, and all were male, as the women had been entertained several hours earlier.

When they were duly seated, every table fully occupied by its quota of eight, Lai Pek and his son filled all the expectant wineglasses and, as the various courses appeared in ritualistic order, the guests plied their chopsticks with decorous slowness. Quiet conversation was maintained, so no one had to shout in order to make himself heard. In the intervals between his solicitous care for the comfort of his honoured guests, Lai Pek seated himself at a table that accommodated, among others, Tow Lia, Heow Tu, and Beng Hu, the presence of the last affording the greatest gratification to him.

"Marriage," said the portly Heow Tu, who was in his proper element at such a function as this, "is the only rational aim of life. Everybody loves a wedding, even if only as a spectator. You see nothing but smiling faces at every doorstep when a bride passes along a street."

"True, true," murmured Beng Hu in appreciation.

"It does not become us to talk about our own marriages, which, in my case at any rate, took place ages ago," heartily laughed Heow Tu. "But next in importance to getting married oneself is living to see a son do so." He turned to Lai Pek with an ingenuous smile. "Your son and new daughter-in-law make an enchanting pair. A very enchanting pair."

"Golden words flow from your generous politeness," replied Lai Pek, joy radiating from his face.

"I have never attended such a splendid wedding before," said the jovial Heow Tu, "although it has been my undeserved lot to enjoy some that were at the time widely praised."

Lai Pek, speechless with delight, refilled the glasses of those near him.

The banquet dragged on and became noisier. Several of the guests, either because indulgence in liquor was rare, though on such a convivial occasion they felt compelled to behave recklessly or because glass after glass went down their throats, became drunk. When the symptoms grew alarming, before they could proceed to any distressing behaviour in the abandonment of their senses, they were conveyed home as quietly as possible.

"Look at the wine devil," pointed Tow Lia. "He looks as if he is going to fall down unconscious."

"At such a joyful celebration as this," said Heow Tu, who had consumed enough for three men and still retained his normal faculties, without the slightest indecorum in either speech or manner, "a man may drink as much as he likes, though I think it is absurd to end a happy evening in so inconvenient a fashion."

A drunken guest collapsed at that moment and had to be supported and propelled along to a carriage by two friends.

"You have hardly drunk anything, Mr. Sin," remarked Heow Tu.

"I am afraid if I go on much longer I'll fall into the condition of that man." He was nibbling red melon seeds and had collected an impressive pile of husks beside him.

"We'll carry you home, if you should happen to do anything of the sort," offered Heow Tu benevolently.

“Thank you,” said Beng Hu hastily. “I couldn’t consider putting you to any such trouble, which might tax even your patience.”

“I am always ready to help a friend in any extremity,” remarked Heow Tu, with an exemplary, generous smile.

“I think we must leave now,” stated Tow Lia to Lai Pek.

“It’s still early,” replied Lai Pek gravely.

“We must sleep off the effects of repletion,” responded Tow Lia still more gravely. “May you live to see a hundred grandsons!”

Heow Tu and Beng Hu murmured equally appropriate wishes.

As Lai Pek accompanied them to the door, Tow Lia exclaimed, “What a starry night!”

Chapter 22

The Slump

A year swiftly came and went, bringing in its wake an economic disaster that produced general distress in the once-prosperous country, where nature and man had smiled in unison. The staple products, rubber and tin, two equally important blessings, one liquid and the other solid, one from a tree and the other from the ground, fell in price to a level unprecedented for its severity, affecting to no small extent every branch of industry and commerce. All persons, wealthy or otherwise, found themselves hard hit, and trade became inert to an alarming degree. The slump became a favourite topic of conversation, and little else occupied the thoughts of merchants, many of whom were reduced to absolute indigence. Misery was rampant, and despair relentlessly forced its way into the most sanguine faces.

Lai Pek was among the victims of this terrible menace, which was hardly comprehensible at first, yet proved relentless and difficult to dispel. He had never thoroughly recovered from the unpleasant effects of Sin Beng Hu's fierce competition, which had, in days gone by, produced in him great anger and disgust and had made him, willy-nilly, conceive a hatred for his rival, although hatred was a rare phenomenon with him. True, they had come to a mutual reconciliation in good time and were no longer rivals; nevertheless, the mere existence of Beng Hu's large concern still took away a part of Lai Pek's former business. In addition, he had lost some capital before they reached terms of agreement. Another contributing cause to his misfortune was his miserable rubber estate, which no one would purchase and which lay in idleness for such a long period of time that by the time people had forgotten about possible encounters with tigers and could be induced to work there, it was in an unseemly condition and resembled a jungle. By the time the grass was mown down at considerable cost, the great fall in price rendered the rubber of no profit whatever, and tapping the trees might as well be stopped for any good it produced. To prevent the land from growing wild again, he had to support a few mowers. The estate was the curse of his life, he thought bitterly.

His business came almost to a standstill, to a degree he had never previously experienced. From one day's end to another, a mere handful of customers entered his shop—not affluent ones at that but seedy-looking individuals who haggled over the most trifling purchases with a persistence so exasperating that he lost his temper at times and uttered some rude remarks, resulting in the permanent loss of their patronage. He was forced to reduce the size of his staff, causing a keen pang of self-reproach about driving into hardship people who had worked for him a considerable number of years and whom he personally liked. Month after month his balance-sheet showed an increasing tendency to swell on the adverse side, in a highly agonising fashion, till finally he was on the verge of bankruptcy.

He worked day and night to remedy this monstrous state of affairs; he devised plans that at first seemed feasible enough but turned out utterly futile, sometimes actually accelerating his downward rush to ruin. His brain never ceased to work, even in the middle of the night, when, restlessly shifting his body from side to side, he sighed or groaned softly. The morning found him dull, with drooping eyelids and a miserable headache no pills could cure. When he was in the shop, he would sit for long hours with his head bent over the counter, a picture of dejection. Occasionally he raised his head to look at the goods with obvious repugnance.

Although he never was very particular with regard to personal appearance, he now completely neglected it. A straggly beard became a prominent feature, as he was too preoccupied even to look at a razor with favour. His puckered brow gave evidence of engrossing thought, and his eyes—once as sharp as needles, seeming to penetrate through whatever they rested upon, beaming watchfulness as they glanced and twinkled in all directions, observing everything—were now listless. He lost the prosperous fullness of his cheeks, which became sunken, hollow, and extraordinarily pale. When he walked, his arms were locked behind his back; his formerly dignified figure stooped, his head bowed, and his gait was a slow shuffle.

His temperament was transformed. No longer was he urbane and smiling; no longer was he disposed to be amiable towards everybody. All things seemed to aggravate him; he became prone to taking umbrage at any trifle. His whole attitude, instead of expressing his earnest desire to oblige any person who approached him, was now rather offensive. He had lost his smooth easiness; morose irritability was the order of the day. In the bosom of his family, he was glum and silent, and Mrs. Lee, in order to avoid an unpleasant bark from him at some remark that before had seemed perfectly innocent, found it her best policy to refrain from speech as much as possible. He would not accept any consolation at all—it only made him distinctly sarcastic, causing the speaker to depart in confusion with the unappealing feeling that he was a hypocrite.

Gone was his complacent confidence in himself. His ancestors had deserted him—there was no doubt about that. His mind absolutely ceased to glory in its supposed wisdom, a belief Lai Pek had tenaciously cherished for a vast number of years. He was a miserable failure, and his will gradually degenerated into vacillating impotence. The common saying, "A rooster tries to fly like a phoenix," forcibly presented itself to his mind as singularly applicable to him. He had always pursued only one creed, which was brimful of simplicity: he had concentrated on practical success, his enthusiasm not allowed to shift from that goal, like a stately ship that does not veer from its predestined course and steadily journeys onward. The horizon of his life had never been clouded with fanciful extras: no curiosity about other subjects ever brushed its wings against his mind. He revered his own success, and that was enough for him. Now success had become a farce, and he sank in his own estimation as inexorably as a stone cast into a pond sinks to the bottom. After all his lifetime of strenuous exertions, this was the result, this tragic failure and misery.

He was sick of life—it held no further attractions for him. What indeed was the use of spending a few extra years as everyone's laughingstock, enduring a beggarly existence? It would be much better to liberate his soul from his body, and, using whatever remnants of his fortune remained, be buried with a seemly degree of pomp and the necessary rites, so that his spirit might wander to the nether regions in a pleasant manner, not in a distressing condition of penury. His mind began to ponder the best method of ending his being as painlessly as possible; he feverishly balanced the respective advantages of jumping into a pond, dangling at the end of a rope, cutting his throat, or swallowing a quantity of some potent poison. But he could not bring himself to any decisive action, for he shrank from the horror of such a desperate deed.

"What are you always thinking about?" asked Mrs. Lee plaintively.

"What is that to you?" he retorted savagely.

"If you were to tell me your troubles sometimes, I might be able to help you."

"You? Help me?" he sneered with ferocious sarcasm.

"We are no worse off than many of our neighbours. I am sure this slump will soon come to an end."

"That is what you believe, in your ignorance. And I see no reason why I should feel consoled because there are others in the same plight. You had better keep your undesired words to yourself. They only drive me mad."

He could not tolerate his wife, who seemed nothing but an encumbrance and a torture to his nerves, and he was conscious of extreme disgust with her and her trifling prattle, which never contained an ounce of sense. He was amazed that he could have lived with her for so many years and ever have imagined her to be a pleasant companion.

He began again to contemplate suicide in earnest and came to the conclusion that the best thing to do was quietly to slide into one of the lakes on the verge of the town and disappear beneath its surface without making any commotion. The more he pondered such a prospect, the more it enticed him. Night was the proper time; no one would be around to interfere or to make a precipitate jump out of fear of detection an awkward necessity. He wanted a quiet death that would appear the result of an accident; self-destruction was not exactly a reputable mode of departure from the world, and in his last moments of existence, he must maintain his dignity.

Without telling anybody where he was going, he left his house when evening had just merged into darkness and a crescent moon was visible in the cloudless heavens. He looked neither right nor left, but with brooding eyes bent over the ground, he steadily walked along unfrequented roads till he reached the lakes. No acquaintance encountered him on the way except Heow Tu, who chanced to be taking a constitutional, swinging his portentous walking stick as he passed Lai Pek on the other side of the road. The portly, good-natured Heow Tu was about to utter some words of greeting, but noticing that Lai Pek was very much preoccupied and absolutely unaware of his proximity and recollecting the snub he received once for giving unwelcome words of goodwill, Heow Tu didn't speak. Very sad, he thought, that a friend whom he had known for so many years should be reduced to such a melancholy state, but what could be done to help him? He shook his head in sadness and went straight home, having lost all his zest for the stroll.

Lai Pek lingered on the wet, grassy edge of a tolerably big lake and gazed into its rippling water, swept by a cool breeze. Except for a flickering lamp some distance away on the side of the road, the place was dark, and no other human being seemed to be in sight. Far away, scattered lights gleamed among the dark masses of the hills, silhouetted against the sky.

Now that the fulfilment of his desire was imminent, Lai Pek was still very irresolute. The invigorating freshness of the air somewhat eased his clouded mind, and once again he reluctantly reviewed the pros and cons of the action he was about to commit. Yes, there was no use prolonging a miserable life, but it was rather hideous to be a corpse, floating in the water. He had once seen a drowned man, and what a sight he had been, bloated beyond recognition. What a sorry spectacle he would be when he was fished out the next day, perhaps! Life held nothing more in store for him, but why shouldn't he shoulder his burden bravely? A hint of his former confidence crept into his heart. His luck might return, though that was a very remote possibility. Still, one never knew. That a man like him, after a meritorious life, should come to such an end was pitiable. Then he thought of something that finally made him decide to forgo his attempt at self-destruction. In his weakened constitution, he could not last very much longer; he would soon die a natural death, one so much more comforting than an untimely act. He had better wait for that occasion as nobly as he could. For the first time in many months he smiled a faint smile, a smile indicative of his new resolution.

Then his foot slipped. He was standing on the very brink of the lake, and as he turned to walk back, he lost his balance. With a splash he tumbled into the dark, cold water and disappeared beneath its surface. When his head rose up again, he instinctively raised a loud cry of distress, a cry which rent the silent night. Not many yards away, seated on a bench, was a man engaged in calm enjoyment of the fresh air, screened from sight by a tree. When the man heard the terrified voice issuing from the darkness, he rushed towards the spot and without a moment's hesitation jumped into the lake, as in the niggardly light of the street lamp he saw the unfortunate Lai Pek floundering in the water. With unerring precision he reached him in two strokes, and despite Lai Pek's frantic struggles, dragged him ashore.

Lai Pek lay on the grass for a time, collecting his strength and recovering from his shock. When he opened his eyes and saw his rescuer, he smiled a pathetic smile.

"What happened?" asked the man sympathetically, wringing out his completely soaked and muddy clothes.

"I slipped and fell," murmured Lai Pek.

"What were you doing here?"

"I was just enjoying the fresh air."

"Come. Let me take you home quickly. You must feel very cold," said the kindly stranger.

When Lai Pek reached his house, as crestfallen and miserable-looking as a wet fowl, his family was gathered in the parlour. Mrs. Lee was anxious, for although her husband had been behaving oddly for months past, she could not help wondering where he had gone; he was not wont to be absent at night. She was horrified to see him return in such a bedraggled state, and when she learned from his rescuer what had actually happened—Lai Pek was curiously quiet, averse to talking in his exhausted condition—she gave a painful cry of dismay and proceeded to bustle around him. He preserved a stony silence, though he was no longer churlish. Dread gripped her heart; she did not think it probable that he could have been really enjoying the fresh air when the accident occurred, because that particular type of wholesome recreation had never appealed to him at all, and he had hardly ever visited the lakes, even by day. She did not reveal her suspicions about the truth to him—a new and sinister element of tragedy had pervaded her world and filled her with inexpressible horror.

Chapter 23

Between Life and Death

The next day Lai Pek fell ill. It commenced with a cold and a splitting headache, sufficient in themselves to make a man lose all interest in life. He soon experienced a chill that lasted half an hour; his teeth chattered and his body trembled lamentably. A fever immediately ensued—not one of gentle warmth but of fiery vigour. He took to bed, a wretched, disillusioned man, persuaded that his much desired end was now within hailing distance. He coughed incessantly, a dry, hacking cough; his breathing was laboured and rapid, most uncomfortable to behold, and he lay on his right side, which was tortured with acute pain.

Sum Goh duly called in a doctor with the best local reputation to diagnose and prescribe for his father's illness. The expert healer, after applying a stethoscope all over the patient's chest and tapping it with his fingers, announced the disease as lobar pneumonia, the right lung being affected. He ordered complete rest and a fluid diet and prescribed some invaluable drugs, including a stimulant for the heart and a sleeping draught at night; for the pain, a poultice was to be applied.

Mrs. Lee was worried beyond measure. Besides nursing him tenderly, she tried everything she could think of to bring her husband back to a priceless state of health, thus placing her own health in jeopardy by neglecting the proper amount of slumber, for she had always been a heavy sleeper who could not be awakened, as Lai Pek once said, by a thief making a loud commotion near her ears. Not satisfied with the doctor called in by Sum Goh, and in order to make doubly sure, she invited a physician skilled in the ancient traditional methods for curing a host of aliments. After feeling Lai Pek's pulse with requisite gravity for nearly a quarter of an hour, thereby learning everything about his condition, he wrote a lengthy prescription and, receiving his fee enclosed in red paper, went off with a delighted countenance. Taking the prescription to a druggist's shop, Mrs. Lee obtained the medicine, a huge parcel, of which a certain quantity was boiled in a pot of water, and she brought a good-sized bowl of the concoction to her husband three times a day. Lai Pek was strangely submissive, doing whatever he was told and accepting both varieties of treatment with equal impartiality. Luckily, however, after a couple of days of literally saturating himself with drugs, he was rescued by Sum Goh, who, thinking of the precept about too many cooks spoiling the broth, and pitying his father for having to swallow so much unpalatable stuff, sternly prevented his mother from administering any more bowls of the boiling liquid. Following an indignant outburst, Mrs. Lee consented to her son's suggestion after he pointed out the incontestable truth that if his father took so much medicine, he would be unable to digest any food at all. However efficacious the medicine might have been, lack of proper nutrition would be far more dangerous and produce consequences the opposite of those desired. She was not bereft of other potent consolations though—she daily offered prayers to Heaven for her husband's recovery, and the household deity also obtained his share of worship, accompanied by burning candles and incense sticks.

As for Lai Pek, he was quite apathetic about his fate and lay still most of the time, watching with lacklustre eyes whatever greeted his vision. Feeling certain he would never rise again, he thought it better not to sully his last moments with displays of fretfulness over the question of taking the drugs, which could have no effect on him, whether for good or for bad. He was pleased that death should come to him in this gentle, peaceful fashion instead of by a violent suicide. During the long hours of repose, his mind vaguely wandered over many fields of thought, and he reviewed the experiences of his entire life—his poverty-stricken boyhood, his youthful struggles, with all their ups and downs, and the following period of manhood, crowned with glorious success. He was assailed with self-pity; after all, he had done nothing to deserve his ill-starred end. He had never committed a crime and had occasionally contributed to charity. On the other hand, he had known many corrupt people who had lived and died in opulence and splendour, people who ought to have been hanged. What a trick fate was playing on him, to be sure!

Friends dropped in to see him. His cantankerous behaviour during the last few months had rather estranged them; but they were aware of his calamities and, though they had no alternative other than to keep away from him, they bore him no enmity in return. Most of them were in difficulties themselves and could not very well offer him any help; besides, it was very doubtful whether he would have accepted, if offered. Sometimes, over a game of mahjong, Tow Lia and Heow Tu discussed his affairs, and then one of them would observe that the poor fellow was to be pitied. Concluding their remarks with simultaneous sighs, expressive of the profoundest sorrow, they became absorbed in their game once more. They, as well as other friends, paid visits to Lai Pek's bedside when they heard of his serious illness, stayed for a few moments, expressed the hope that he would get well soon, and tiptoed out of the room. Lai Pek received them with a faint smile and mumbled a few appropriate words in reply.

Among the visitors was Sin Beng Hu, who came on the second day of his illness. After inquiring of Sum Goh about Lai Pek's condition, he gingerly entered the sickroom, where all the windows were open to admit the fresh air. He was surprised to find Lai Pek in such a wasted condition; he had been away from Lanta for about a month on a pleasurable holiday and had thus not seen him during that time. The economic slump had affected him but little, though even he could not entirely escape its ominous influence, and he remained the same in person and character as when he first came to that town. He was as grave as ever, and he quickly subdued his involuntary surprise and remarked, "You look ill, Mr. Lee. What has come over you?"

"I think I am dying," said Lai Pek wearily.

"How could you talk like that? You are sure to recover, of course, though your appearance certainly suggests that you have been neglecting your health. You have not been worrying unduly about business, have you?"

Lai Pek shook his head and turned his face away.

"I hope you don't do anything of the sort. The slump is certain to come to an end soon. Until then, if you don't mind, I'll be glad to give you any help you need. You mustn't let yourself feel depressed over a temporary hardship. We men of business should always be prepared to triumph over difficulties. Think of the joy of struggle!"

A renewed light of enthusiasm glimmered for a fraction of a second in Lai Pek's eyes and then promptly subsided.

"Do you know what I would do if I were you?" continued the encouraging Beng Hu. "I would be as cheerful as a bird and forget all cares." As he said these words, his mien became graver than ever. "I would cultivate the will to be hale and strong again. It's always a great pleasure to know that one has safely come through an illness. It makes one feel that life lies in one's hands and that one has achieved a great victory. And then, when I was well, I would reorganise my business to meet the present conditions and tide it over the existing crisis."

"I'll try to follow your advice," murmured Lai Pek, closing his eyes.

Beng Hu saw that he was tired, and after a few more consolatory words, he left him to his repose.

Low Tua Sai presented his kindly, wizened face the next morning. Seating himself by the patient's bedside, he first suppressed a tiny cough and then looked as uncomfortable as if he were the person afflicted with disease. They glanced at one another once or twice without saying anything, and Tua Sai took off his spectacles and wiped them with slow, deliberate movements, giving him the air of one performing a ritual. He passed his hand over his thin hair, scratched his ears and elbows, and then finally opened his mouth. "It's curious you should have gone to the lakes for a walk at night. Of course, some people go there regularly, but I never do. You weren't fond of the area, if I remember aright."

"Some evil spirit must have drawn me to the spot," was the gloomy answer.

"Probably," agreed Tua Sai, feeling a tinge of fear. "Otherwise your unlucky accident would be inexplicable."

Lai Pek stared at the ceiling in vacant silence.

"I fell into a river once," continued Tua Sai reminiscently, "and knocked my head against a stone. That's how I got this scar." He pointed to a slight scar that ran across his brow, but Lai Pek wasn't looking. "Very miserable I felt when I scrambled out of the water. You did not fall against any hard substance, did you?"

"No," said Lai Pek feebly.

"That's one thing lucky. As for your illness, you'll soon get over it. Cheer up! There's nothing to worry about. I shall see you well soon."

The little man walked on tiptoe out of the room and gently closed the door behind him, his exit unnoticed by Lai Pek, who was still absorbed in contemplation of the ceiling, which seemed to be affording him great entertainment.

His illness continued its course. The sputum he coughed up was tenacious and rusty coloured, and his breathing was so short, rapid, and noisy and took so much effort that it seemed as if he must immediately perish from exhaustion. His temperature fluctuated one or two degrees every day but remained very high; his forehead was like fire and his skin dry and pungent. He ate only a bit, slept fitfully and uneasily, was extremely restless, and now and then kicked his feet against the mattress impatiently.

He grew delirious and muttered all kinds of horrible words, like *devils* and *tigers*, which nearly threw Mrs. Lee into a fit with terror. To the horror of Mrs. Lee he would point his finger rigidly towards the door and, addressing some invisible demon, loudly command him to remove his unwelcome presence or scream and seem to kick away an imaginary beast that was on the point of devouring him. He had frequent dreams, not the blissful dreams that a man lying awake in the morning likes to recollect, trying to piece together the gossamer fragments; not a beautiful dream, like that of Coleridge about the great Kubla Khan's *sunny pleasure-dome with caves of ice*, but hideous ones, which were best forgotten as soon as possible. Once while he was apparently asleep, he suddenly jumped out of bed, exclaiming that a hidden scorpion lurked, trying to sting him, and he only resigned himself to reluctant quietness after Mrs. Lee's coaxing powers were brought into service.

On the fifth day of his illness his delirium passed away, and that night he slept profoundly, untroubled by a single dream. The next morning found him weak and exhausted, but his eyes no longer held a haunted look, and he could think more or less clearly, though the pain in his chest rendered thought irksome. Mrs. Lee came in, a radiant smile replacing the anxious, sad expression she had worn since Lai Pek's accident. The latter noticed the strange smile but was too languid even to wonder at it, much less to ask her the cause. After he had swallowed his medicine and she had made him as comfortable as possible on the bed, she remarked, "I have good news to tell. Last night Gek Kim gave birth." Lai Pek opened his eyes a bit wider but said nothing. "Yes, and a boy too. And so fine!" exclaimed Mrs. Lee enthusiastically. "Why, you are a grandfather now!"

As she clasped her hands rapturously, Lai Pek closed his eyes to ponder over the sudden revelation. When Mrs. Lee thought he had fallen asleep, he slowly opened them again, and there was a smile on his lips, weak indeed, but obviously reflecting a certain measure of joy. He turned towards her, and no penetrating intellect was needed to understand that he was desirous of further information.

"Both the mother and the child are quite well. Such a remarkable baby. So charming." She did not specify exactly in what respect he was remarkable or charming. "You must now get well as speedily as possible. You must see him soon."

All that day Lai Pek lay thinking of the newborn baby. He was a grandfather, an extremely lucky man. He could already hear the joyful congratulations that would be showered on him by the townsfolk. What blessed things children were! He could still remember his ecstasy when Sum Goh himself was first born. How restless Lai Pek had been as he rushed to and fro, not knowing what to do, impatiently waiting for the moment when a shrill cry would announce the new arrival. He did not feel quite as elated when his other children came. But to be a grandfather! That was an experience he had never tasted before. He was an ancestor: he saw himself at the head of an interminable line of descendants. He must live—must live a few more years, surrounded by little children calling him grandfather. It was ridiculous that he should die before the age of fifty! Extremely ridiculous!

Then he thought of his financial troubles, and sadness crept into his eyes. But this was quickly replaced by confidence. Why should he despair? What Sin Beng Hu said was quite right—struggle was in itself a bliss. He had heartily embraced the glory of strife in his youth, and now with his riper knowledge of men and things, he should not find it so difficult to get out of a temporary mess. He had succumbed from weakness, egregiously unworthy of a man of strong character; he had admitted defeat after only a few months of misery. He was averse to suicide and death—even in poverty this world still contained some good.

He now began to contemplate with deep interest the progress of his illness, which was certainly a serious one. He had never before suffered such a prostrating attack of any sort. He must do all he could to conserve his strength; he must banish worry from his mind. For four days after his new resolution, his illness continued, as severe as ever. Except that he was no longer subject to delirium, the symptoms continued unabated. Then, suddenly, sweat oozed through his pores with tremendous profusion, steeping his clothes and bedding in such a deluge of water, one might have been tempted to imagine such an amount could never be contained within a single human body, however bulky that body might have been. Together with this phenomenon, his temperature dropped at a prodigious rate, with the result that in fifteen hours it had fallen from its previous dizzy height to a level below normal, where it remained for some time, and he felt exhausted. The other symptoms fled the now uninviting abode; the multifarious bacteria, which had been having such a splendid time inside him, were now definitely vanquished.

His convalescence was of unusually short duration. He still lay in bed most of the day, indulging his fancy with sanguine plans for the re-emergence of prosperity, plans he would put in practise the moment he was strong enough to begin work anew. He wondered how he could ever have thought it possible that he was lost forever, that life held nothing more for him. And when he dreamed at night, it was a marvellously pleasant dream of a thriving business and numerous grandchildren. Sometimes he laughed softly to himself, to the consternation of Mrs. Lee, who fancied that he was under attack by some peculiar form of delirium, since he vouchsafed no information regarding his outbursts. The first thing he asked of her every morning was whether the baby was well and whether he was getting plump or not. On receiving her reply in the affirmative, he invariably congratulated both himself and his happy spouse on their luck, remarking that they were without a doubt under the special protection of Providence; otherwise, a grandchild—and a grandson at that—would not have fallen to their lot. He then laughed a short laugh and fell into a reverie.

Chapter 24

The Completion of the Moon

Abundant joy reigned in the house of Lai Pek, who had recovered from his severe illness and was well and active, through he still had some way to go before he could be said to be in complete possession of adequate strength, for it was the one-month anniversary of the birth of the son of Sum Goh and Gek Kim. A feast was held to celebrate this completion of the moon, as the occasion was called, and gifts for the baby were sent by relatives and friends.

Never was there a happier person anywhere in the world than the admirable Gek Kim. Her radiant smile was now more enchanting than ever, and her visible pleasure in her new exalted position made the beholder's heart vibrate joyfully in response. She delighted everybody, and in whatever capacity she stood with respect to any particular individual, whether as daughter, daughter-in-law, wife, niece, or friend, she behaved with becoming propriety. She was without exaggeration a genuine pearl, as Mrs. Lee said, and upon whose judgment could greater reliance be placed than that of a mother-in-law?

The baby was dressed in splendid new clothes; in fact, his wardrobe was remarkably large and included contributions from various relatives. Several months previously, acting in the full belief that the baby would be a boy, Mrs. Low had in her idle hours sewed quite a goodly number of suits for him.

Whenever anyone questioned her on her unlikely certainty concerning the sex of her yet unborn grandchild, she retorted that she possessed infallible knowledge on the subject, as the gods themselves gave her the information in answer to her prayers.

The hair that had steadily accumulated on the baby's head was completely shorn for the anniversary. The barber called in for the purpose wished to use an old razor to accomplish the task; he declared that a razor used on a baby who was being shaved for the first time could never be used again. But Sum Goh, fearing that an old razor might not be sharp enough and could conceivably be toxic on account of rust, bought a new one himself. The barber, though he thought it unusual for money to be wasted in that way, raised no objection to the change, because he still received the additional payment he expected, should he be required to use his worn-out instrument, which would then have to be discarded. The work was performed with a dexterous skill, which evoked the admiration of the family, who gathered round to watch the interesting operation, marvelling at the child's quietness. The barber then departed with a pleased smile.

The feast was well attended, and every visitor showered congratulations on the family, of whom Lai Pek was the principal and most gratified recipient. Blessings on the baby were varied and numerous. *May he grow up good and glorious*; *may he be an honour to his parents*; *may he reach a venerable age*—such auspicious wishes buzzed throughout the house. Mrs. Lee, holding the baby in her arms, proudly presented him to each guest, beaming with joy at every congratulatory remark and expression of admiration.

His name was decided upon at a solemn family meeting.

"The name of the boy," began Lai Pek, opening the discussion, "should reflect a favourable omen. Of course, he will grow up wonderful and meritorious, no matter what we choose to call him, but still, a fine-sounding name is more pleasant."

"What about Singing Bird?" advanced Tua Sai. The little man was a bit greyer and his features were rather more wizened; but his accommodating disposition, ever ready to oblige a person in order that harmony might prevail, remained unimpaired. At first he had found it difficult to bear the departure of his daughter from under his roof, and he sorely missed her presence. The house, as he repeatedly told himself, was strangely deprived of light and music. Nevertheless, after he reflected upon the inevitable necessity of such an event, he gradually resigned himself to the altered situation. He ultimately consoled himself with the thought that circumstances were no worse, for she lived nearby and could, and did, come to see him pretty frequently.

"That," said Lai Pek with due gravity, "is a graceful name. But I am afraid it's inappropriate. It might apply better to a girl. Singing is not a very praiseworthy accomplishment." He turned towards Tua Sai with a conciliatory smile, intimating that he did not mean to give any offence by his objection to the suggestion.

"You are right," said Tua Sai in handsome agreement. "I have always liked singing birds, and I just thought that the name would sound sweet. What do you propose he should be called?"

"I think Always Happy is the best name. It is the most suitable, as I am convinced that the child will be of a happy disposition. The word *happy* includes everything: wealth, health, long life, reputation, and all other factors that make existence desirable."

He concluded in triumph and looked around for approval. At that moment the baby, for no apparent reason whatever, began to cry loudly and continued the display for five minutes before he was lulled to sleep again by Gek Kim. Those present instinctively looked at Lai Pek humorously and he felt abashed. Before he could proceed to say anything more, however, Gek Kim remarked, "What about Bright Fire? I can give no special reason for its choice, except that it sounds quite nice."

"Excellent!" chimed in Sum Goh. "Both words are propitious. May his life be like a bright fire, glorious and splendid!"

Sum Goh was just as devoted to Gek Kim as ever, even though they had been married for one year, during which period no quarrel worth mentioning had ever arisen between them to mar their blissful concord.

Everyone approved the name and observed that it was uncommonly fine, except Lai Pek, who was not wholeheartedly in its favour, as he dearly wished to have something to do with the name of his first grandchild.

"Fire is not wholly beneficent in its effects," he demurred; "it may burn down a house. Bright Sun is better. The sun shines high above the world and is wholly good."

"I agree," said Gek Kim pleasantly. "The word *sun* is ten times better than the word *fire*."

The amendment met with hearty approval from all members of the family, and the child was therefore dubbed Bright Sun. After this tremendously important matter had reached a satisfactory conclusion, they felt more at ease and proceeded to discuss other topics, as a gathering of this sort was too agreeable to break up in a hurry.

"The baby must be brought up very carefully," said Lai Pek, who was now extremely fond of hearing his own voice. "He must lack nothing that can make him a perfect man. The two most important things to consider are sound health and respectable behaviour. We want people to say, 'Here is a boy whose parents have known how to govern properly!' Many boys nowadays are thoroughly spoilt."

"Very true," interposed Tua Sai with a sympathetic expression. "I have come across some children whose conduct was outrageous. And they were not orphans; their parents had no sense. Of course the saying is true, 'The venomous tiger does not eat its offspring.' But it's mistaken affection to allow children to run wild."

The subject of correct behaviour was finished. Lai Pek, never in more buoyant spirits, which may have been attributable to the fine weather, the memorable occasion, the restoration of his health and renewed hope, began again after a short pause, "The changes of life are extremely curious. Not so long ago I was also a baby. Then, without my having anything to do with the matter, I grew up to be a big boy. When I reached that entrancing stage, what I liked best was to sit on a branch high above the ground, munching a guava. Soon I became a man and had to struggle for a livelihood. The years passed, bringing all sorts of changes, and now I am a grandfather. What will happen in the next twenty years, if I live so long? Perhaps I shall be a great-grandfather."

"The cycle of life from birth to death is certainly very amazing," agreed the amiable Tua Sai. "I sometimes wonder how I have come to have grey hair."

"The gradual change in the person is the strangest of all mysteries," concluded Lai Pek.

When the day came to a close, the night was soothingly charming, presenting a limpid, silvery moon that softly and harmoniously illuminated the floating clouds, shedding its radiance on the world below. The cool breezes whispered through the trees, tall and majestic, that lay in shadow by the side of the road. The flickering lamps contributed glamour to the scene.

Lai Pek sat in a chair in front of his house, serene, happily smoking his pipe. Memory is the closet of experience. He softly released the latch of that closet and tenderly looked into its contents. He considered his past and found it satisfactory. In the present, he found no cause for excessive sorrow. Proceeding into the future, he felt that it was rosy. But, practical man that he was, he interrupted his pleasant reverie as soon as the clock struck ten, for going to bed early so as to conserve his invaluable energy was one of his favourite maxims. Entering the house, he carefully locked the door behind him and walked upstairs at a comfortable pace.

About the Author

Born around the time of the foundation of the Republic of China, in the former English colony of British Malaya, Tan Kheng Yeang was educated in an English school. His father was from China but had emigrated to Malaya and had become a successful businessman, involved in various activities, including as a rubber merchant. From his early days the author was interested in literature and philosophy and as his interest evolved to science, he decided to study civil engineering at the University of Hong Kong, as he felt he needed a practical career.

After the Japanese occupied Hong Kong, he fled to free China where he found work in an office constructing roads and later an airfield in Guangxi Province. After the war ended in 1945, he returned to Malaya and became an engineer in the City Council of Georgetown, Penang. After his retirement, he worked as an engineering consultant. He is the author of twelve books that reflect the broad range of his interests and talents.